Secrets That Lie Between my Thighs 2

A novel by Lady Lissa & Shelli Marie

Last chapter from book 1
Trashelle

That fool Jose wouldn't stop stalking me! After he came at me with that gun, I was spooked. Once inside the apartment, he threw me on the sofa and started going off. He literally looked like a crazy man coming unglued before me. I didn't know what that man was going to do to me, so I slowly crept my hand near my bag.

When I felt what I was looking for, I squeezed it and gently pulled it out. When he came in my face screaming, I quickly attached the taser to his genitals. Never had I seen a man fall to the ground faster than that man. He literally looked like he was frying.

By the time I removed the 800,000 volts taser from his nuts, he wasn't moving but he was moaning, so I knew he was alright. But that bitch needed medical attention ASAP.

I quickly dialed 911 and gave the dispatcher my address. I told her I needed the police because an intruder had been holding me at gunpoint.

"Is the suspect still on the premises?"

"Yes, but he ain't a threat no more!"

"What do you mean ma'am?"

"I mean, you need to send an ambulance because I fried his ass with my taser," I said.

"I'll alert the paramedics that you need assistance."

"Please do," I remarked.

It didn't take long for the cops and paramedics to arrive. They were able to treat Jose on the spot, but then it looked like the cops were about to release him. I wasn't about to let that happen.

"Are you crazy?! You're not gonna arrest him?" I asked.

"He said it was just a big misunderstanding," the officer said in his Spanish accent.

A misunderstanding? That muthafucka had pulled a gun on me! He tried to attack me! There was nothing misunderstood on my part. The part that I wasn't clear on was how they just let him go!

Yeah, I'm freaked the hell out!

"The hell it was! I was held at gunpoint!" I shrieked.

"Where is the gun?" the cop asked.

"Right there!" I pointed to the gun on the floor where Jose laid a little while ago.

"That's not my gun!" Jose said.

"LIAR!!" I yelled.

The officer picked up the gun and put it in a plastic bag. He didn't mark evidence on it or anything, so I wondered what he was going to do with it.

Jose started speaking in Spanish to the officer, who turned to me looking confused. "What the hell are you looking at me for? Arrest him!"

"Ma'am, Mr. Hernandez said if you don't make any more trouble for him, he won't press charges on you for assault," the cop said.

"PRESS CHARGES ON ME?! FOR ASSAULT?!"

"Well, you did admit to using the taser on him..."

"IN SELF DEFENSE!!" I yelled angrily. "HE HAD A GUN TO MY HEAD!!"

"He said it's not his gun," the cop said.

"OH MY GOD!! ARE YOU KIDDING ME?!!"

Jose began speaking to him in Spanish again. He turned to me and said, "We are letting Mr. Hernandez go okay? He dun want no trouble! Just you two need to stay away from each other."

"I DON'T WANT HIM NEAR ME!!" I yelled as I rolled my eyes towards Jose. I couldn't believe this shit was breaking down like this right before my eyes. That ass hole was about to walk like he hadn't done nothing wrong.

"It was just a big misunderstanding," Jose said.

"Misunderstanding my ass!" I huffed. "Just get the fuck out of my apartment! DON'T YOU EVER COME BACK HERE AGAIN!!!"

"Mr. Hernandez, you stay away from her and she stay away from you. You okay with that?"

"I'm cool if she cool," Jose said.

"Just get out!" I snarled.

The two of them walked out the door and I paced the floor for a while. With Jose being out on the streets, free to do whatever the fuck he wanted to do, I was too scared to leave out of my house. I was even too scared to go downtown to file for an order of protection. Even though it was only a piece of paper, it would help me if I ended up shooting and killing Jose's retarded ass.

That was definitely going to be the end result if that crazed maniac didn't leave me alone.

As I sat on the sofa with my .22 in hand, I was nervous and scared. Every little sound I heard caused me to jump. That was when I regretted everything that I did to make Tyson leave. Right now, I needed him more than ever but refused to beg him to help me.

The next person that came to mind was Michael. He was the only other person that I had been talking to on the regular. All my family was miles away in Dallas. I had made the move to Houston by myself because I was looking for better career opportunities.

Feeling alone and scared, I began drinking and smoking to calm down. That shit didn't do nothing but make me more paranoid.

"What was that?" I huffed as I went over to the window and peeked out.

As I deemed the coast clear, I closed the blinds and turned around only to nearly jump out of my skin. It was my cell ringing now.

Answering my phone without checking the screen, I heard Jose on the line threatening me for almost getting him locked up and for charging his nuts. Yeah, that nigga was big mad, but that wasn't shit compared to how scared that fool had me!

I'm a tough cookie, but this shit is crazy!

Getting up from the sofa, I began double checking all the windows and doors. "Why are you harassing me?!" I cried trying to figure out why Jose was tripping so hard.

"Because you led me to believe that I was your man..."

"That's my job Jose!" I screamed trying to make him understand that I was a paid escort, not a paid girlfriend! There were boundaries and that dude had crossed every one of them!

"You wanna tell me that shit now when you played me to the left?! You made me fall in love with you only to find out you were a damn ho'! The things you did with me, you probably did with other muthafuckas too!"

"That's my job Jose! To provide a fantasy for my clients!"

"You are a fucking whore and cunt! You played me Trashelle! You fucking played me!"

"It was my job! I was providing a service for someone who was paying me! It was a job!" I repeated over and over to make him understand, but Jose wasn't listening to a word I was saying.

"I love you Trashelle and this is how you do me! I give you the world! Anything you asked and it was yours! Now you want to play me! You think it's okay to play me?!" He just wasn't getting it and kept going on and on.

"It was my job and you need to get on with your life!" I insisted as I continued to make sure my home was secured.

"It was your job to break my heart Trashelle?"

Jose was screaming again and threatening me again. The things he said he would do to me had me shaking like a fucking leaf! This man was really crazy!

"I will gut you like a fish and feed your heart to my dogs!"

"I have a protective order..." I lied.

"You ain't got shit! My brother is a lawyer, my sister is a cop and my mother is a judge! You can't touch me, but I can touch you!"

Hanging up the phone, I began to panic. I even called downtown to see if I could file for the order of protection online.

"Fuck!" I screamed as I hung up the phone in defeat.

I had to go down there and I was not trying to do that shit!

Taking a chance, I went ahead and got dressed to go. It took about an hour to get ready and another hour to convince myself to leave my home.

Paranoid and afraid, I got in my car and backed it out of the garage. Traveling about ten blocks or so, I wondered if I had closed the garage. This was the dumb shit I did almost every time I parked in there.

"Am I losing my mind?" I mumbled as I doubled back and checked.

When I got there, I saw that I hadn't closed it. Without thinking twice about it, I pressed the remote and watched as the garage door lowered until it reached the ground.

In a hurry, I made a U-Turn and headed downtown to file for a protection order. Luckily for me, it only took an hour to get all the paperwork filled out. I was told that Jose would be served with the papers as soon as they could catch up with them.

"Please let this nigga be served so it can be over with soon!" I spoke out in frustration as I made it home and pulled into my garage.

As I got out of my car and went into the house, I immediately smelled something strange and unfamiliar. Quick thinking caused me to ease out my cell just in case I had to call the cops and a weapon just in case I had to protect myself.

Creeping through my house with my phone in one hand and my taser in the other, I combed through every room including the shower, under the beds and in the closets. When my search turned up empty, I breathed a sigh of relief. I walked back to the kitchen and poured a drink in my glass.

One shot of whiskey led to two and then three. That was enough alcohol in my system to have me tired and ready to lay my ass down.

Allowing my guards to drop, I changed my clothes and stretched out on the top of my bed. Suddenly everything started spinning. My head was circling so badly, you would think I was on a fair ride.

Rising up and stumbling a bit, I lifted my head and looked straight ahead towards my open bedroom door. For a split second, I thought I saw a shadow in the hallway and nearly jumped out my slippers.

"Who's there?!" I called out.

Inching out of my bedroom, I went towards the living room. Just as I approached the opening that led to the kitchen, I felt a mighty blow to my chest. Falling to the floor, I felt another one, then another one.

Before I could try to defend myself, Jose came into plain view with my taser in his hand. "You wanna see how this shit feels between your fucking legs?!"

"No!" I yelled, but my voice didn't come out like a yell. After being hit so many times in the chest, I could barely speak. I was in so much damn pain.

Ignoring my cries, he placed the taser against my side and pressed the button. My entire body started jerking and shaking. I had no control over my body as Jose quickly dropped his pants and boxers. Dropping himself on top of mine, he had his way with me while my body continued to shake.

Trying to claw at him was impossible because I still had no control over my limbs. No matter how loud I cried, Jose wouldn't stop.

"No! No! No!" I begged as he entered me over and over raw. The only thing I could think about was getting pregnant or catching an incurable disease, both of which were life sentences.

"Ugh!" Jose grunted as the warm liquid filled my insides.

Feeling sick to my stomach, I quickly turned my head to the side and started vomiting. You think Jose stopped pounding my pussy? No! That nigga didn't get off me until he was finished.

"Help... me..." I cried trying to catch my breath.

Without a care in the world, Jose got up, got his pants on and told me that he would see me again soon then disappeared from my sight like what had just happened didn't mean shit!

Tears flowed down my cheeks and started stinging my skin as I struggled to get off the floor. Traveling straight to the bathroom, I looked in the mirror and started crying louder when I saw the bruises on my face.

Stepping quickly out of the bathroom, I found my cell and called Tyson. Now I was desperately in need of him!

"Tyson! Please! Please! Come help me!" I cried as I began briefly explaining what had happened to me.

Before I could get it all out, I felt a metal object hit the back of my head. It was like my body started falling in slow motion as I yelled out for Tyson. As darkness enveloped me, I slowly felt life creeping from my body. All I could think about was how I got to this point in my life.

How could I be so stupid to sell myself to all those different strange men? How did I not know that Jose was a loose cannon? How the hell did I not see that he was a threat to my life?

Never did I think that my lifestyle I had kept hidden from Tyson would lead me here. Look at me! I didn't know what was going to happen to me. I didn't know how I had ended up here. I just prayed that Tyson would get here in time to save me.

As tears slipped from my eyes, I said a silent prayer for help...

Please God, I need you now more than ever before. Can you get Tyson here quickly? I need him so much. If you save me this time Lord, I promise never to do anything you don't agree with. Please... help... me...

Chapter One

Tyson

When I got the call from Tray, I didn't know what the hell she was calling me about. Last time we spoke, we were done with each other and those stupid games she seemed to be playing... at least I was done. So, imagine my surprise when I saw her number pop up on my screen. But no one was more surprised than I was when I heard her asking for help. As she briefly told me what was going on, all of a sudden, she just stopped talking. I heard a noise in the background like she had hit the floor or something.

"TRAY! TRAY!!" I yelled into the phone. Then the line went dead.

Aw shit! I grabbed my keys and rushed out of the hotel to go check on her. Something wasn't right because as I was driving, I was calling her, but she wasn't answering. What the hell was going on with her?

It took me all of 10 minutes to make it to her crib since my hotel was right down the street. I parked then rushed over to the door and let myself in.

When I entered her place, I found Trashelle on the floor unconscious with her pants and underwear tossed to the side. I immediately dialed 911 as I looked around her place to make sure no one else was here.

After I finished searching her spot, I knelt beside her to try and wake her up. The operator was still on the line and asking me all kinds of questions.

"Is she breathing?"

"Yes!"

"And she's still unconscious?" she asked.

"Yes, she's out cold!" I said, as I reached for a throw that was on the back of the sofa to cover her up with.

"The paramedics and police should be there shortly sir. May I have your name?"

I gave her my name and information.

"What is the victim's name?"

"Trashelle..."

"Can you spell that for me?"

"T-r-a-s-h-e-l-l-e, last name Young!"

Suddenly hearing sirens in the near distant, I stood up and went to the door. Walking outside, I raised my hands as I stood in the driveway, so they wouldn't pass the house up.

Standing there waving, I caught the ambulance driver's attention. Acknowledging me, he nodded and turned into the driveway.

"The paramedics and police are here," I informed the operator.

"Okay. I hope your friend is okay," she said.

"Thanks," I said as I ended the call.

Leading the paramedics and police into the house, I watched as they tried to wake Tray up. I knew that she and I hadn't been on the best of terms, but I never wanted anything like this to happen to her. I mean, who the fuck had assaulted her and why? The police were asking me questions to find out what I knew, but I didn't know shit. I showed them my phone to let them know that she and I were on the phone when I heard a thump in the background.

"I guess whoever was here had knocked her over the head or something," I explained. "I had a feeling that something had happened to her, so I rushed over here from the hotel up the street."

"So, the two of you were on the phone when this happened?" the cop asked.

"Yes! Yes!"

"Did you hear anyone in her home?"

"No, all I heard was something drop to the floor. I figured she was in trouble, so I rushed right over. I had tried calling her back several times, but she didn't pick up. When I got here, I found her like this so called 911 and threw a blanket over her."

The paramedics loaded Tray onto the gurney and began to exit the house. "I need to go with her."

"Can I get your phone number?"

I rattled off my number to him and he handed me a card. "This is the case number and my name and number. If you think of anything that would help with this case, give me a call. We will be by the hospital later," he said.

"Thanks," I said as I rushed out the door.

Since I was told that I couldn't ride in the back of the ambulance, I hopped back in my truck and followed them to the hospital. The whole ride there, I prayed that Tray would be alright. What kind of maggot would do a woman like that? That just went to show that the shit she was doing shouldn't have been done. She should've kept her damn legs closed and her fucking panties on her ass.

Of course, I wasn't blaming Trashelle for this, but she played some part in who she let into her life. She could've avoided all this shit had she just been faithful. I was a good man to Tray and she knew it. Sure, I got a little carried away with Eraina, but that wasn't until I found out what the hell Tray had been up to. If she had kept her legs closed, I would've never slept with Eraina.

As the ambulance pulled into the hospital parking lot, I parked my truck in one of the spots reserved for emergency room patients. As they went in with Tray, I followed behind them. They took her to a room and the doctors started working to try and get her up. After some freaking procedure that took about 10 seconds, her eyes finally fluttered open. I was glad about that because I didn't want anything bad to happen to her.

"Where am I?" she asked as she looked around frightened.

"Ma'am you're in the hospital. I'm Dr. Lyle, can you tell me your name?"

"Trashelle."

"Trashelle do you remember what happened to you?" Dr. Lyle asked.

After briefly closing her eyes, Tray opened them looking more scared than before. Continuing to blink quickly, she began to look around at everyone.

"It's okay. You're in the hospital and you're safe. Nothing is going to happen to you here," Dr. Lyle assured patting her hand. "Can you tell me what happened?"

"Someone hit me on the head..." She reached around and touched the back of her head.

"Do you know who it was?"

"I have an idea."

"You'll want to tell the police when they come down here to question you. So, here's what we're going to do. I'm going to need a CBC, CT scan, urinalysis, and we're going to do a rape kit..."

"Rape kit? I was raped?" Tray asked the doctor.

"We can't say for sure, but this gentleman found you and you didn't have any bottoms on," the doctor said as he pointed to me.

Tray looked at me with tears in her eyes. "You came?"

"Of course, I did. When the line went dead, I had to make sure you were alright," I mumbled as I walked over to her.

Reaching out for my hand, I placed mine in hers and held onto it as she cried. "I'm so sorry Tyson!"

"I know. I know."

"I never meant to hurt you!"

"I know that too. Let's just concentrate on getting you out of here," I said. The last thing I wanted was for the two of us to discuss our personal issues in front of these strangers.

The doctor walked out of the room while the nurse stayed behind. As she reached in one of the cabinets and gave the urine cup to Trashelle, I read her nametag, 'Abby'.

"I can walk you down to the restroom." Nurse Abby leaned to help Tray out of bed but when she noticed that she was dizzy, she immediately sat her back down. "I'll get a wheelchair!"

Nurse Abby left the room and returned a short time later with a wheelchair. Seeing that she was struggling a bit, I helped her get Trashelle into the chair. Opting to stay behind, I watched as Abby wheeled her out the room.

Sitting back down in the room, I got as comfortable as I could while I waited for them return. After about five minutes later I got restless and began pacing but only made it across the room twice before Abby wheeled Tray back in.

Going over to them, I helped Tray get from the wheelchair back in the bed. She still had tears in her eyes.

"Someone will be here shortly to take you to radiology. And the nurse should be here to take your blood in a couple of minutes..."

"What about the rape kit?"

"I will get Dr. Lyle and we will perform it shortly."

"Will it hurt?" Tray asked.

"Not at all. It's just to take DNA samples to give to the police to help them catch whoever did this to you," Abby explained.

"Thank you."

"You're welcome. Be right back," Abby said before walking out the door.

"I can't believe this is happening," Tray sighed heavily as she leaned her head back.

"Who did this to you Tray? What the hell happened?"

"This dude who used to be a client of mine has been stalking me..."

"Stalking you? Are you serious?"

"Yes, I had to get a restraining order and everything, but as you can see, that didn't work. I don't know why he is doing this," she said.

"So, some dude you used to fuck for money has been stalking you? And tonight, he got in the house, knocked you out and took the pussy that he had been paying you for, right?" I asked, finding this shit hard to believe.

"That's exactly what happened. Why are you saying it like you don't believe me or something?"

"I don't know Tray. This shit just sounds crazy," I said.

"It is crazy! That son of a bitch has been harassing and stalking me for weeks!"

"Why didn't you tell me?" I asked.

"How could I? You were so busy fucking your..."

I held up my hand to stop her from embarrassing herself further. "Don't do that! I mean, if you were honest with yourself you would know that you got the ball rolling on that shit!"

"So, it's my fault that you were sleeping with that bitch?"

"Yes! Yes! It is very much your fault! If I hadn't found out all that shit about you fuckin' those other niggas, none of this shit would be happening right now!" I said angrily.

I knew I should've kept my cool because she had been through a lot this evening, but she had me fucked up. She always wanted to point out the shit that I did but always seemed to forget the part she played.

"Tyson!" Tray yelled just as the doctor and nurse walked. Thankfully she couldn't finish responding.

"We will do the rape kit now. Sir, do you mind stepping out for a minute?" Dr. Lyle asked.

"Not a problem. I need some fresh air anyway," I said.

Heading out of the room, I found the nearest exit to stand outside and take in as much fresh air as my lungs could hold in a breath. After about 12 minutes or so, I walked back into the hospital and went back to the room where Tray was at. The room was empty, so my guess was that they came to get her for the CT scan. I just sat in the chair and waited for her to come back.

As I idled there, I thought about calling her mom for her, but then quickly decided against it. Hell, Tray could do that when and if she decided she wanted her mom to know. Her phone had been taken by the police as evidence since someone had smashed it up and shit. I was more than sure it was the person who assaulted her that had busted up her phone.

While waiting and debating my next move, my attention was captured by the door swinging open. It was Tray being brought back in the room.

"It'll take about 45 minutes to an hour before we get all your results back. Just sit tight and we'll be back as soon as we can," Dr. Lyle said.

"How do you feel?" I asked.

"My head hurts. I have a huge lump back there."

"I'm sure it does. Just relax and close your eyes. Maybe the light is what's bothering you."

"Maybe."

Tray closed her eyes and relaxed her head against the pillow. I didn't really want to have a conversation with her because I was tired arguing, so I sat there fidgeting.

Welcoming the distraction as my phone beeped signaling a text message, I pulled it from my pocket and checked to see who it was. It was Eraina.

Eraina: Wya?

Me: Why?

Eraina: I'm at your hotel. We need to talk

Me: I'm not there

Eraina: Well how long will you be? I'll wait

Me: No, you can leave cuz Idk how long I'm gonna be

Eraina: Well you need to come over here. I have something important to talk to you about

Me: We said everything we needed to say last time. I'm handling some business right now

Eraina: This is serious Tyson!!

Slipping my phone back in my pocket after ignoring the last text, I shook my head. This shit wasn't getting us anywhere.

"Was that your girlfriend?"

"She's not my girlfriend!" I responded.

"Whatever Tyson! You know you don't have to stay here, right?" Tray asked.

"Damn! That's the thanks I get for trying to be there for your ass! Shit, you did call my phone yea, or did you forget that shit?"

"No, I remember. It just doesn't seem like you wanna be here. And if that's the case, you can feel free to go."

The doctor walked in a few minutes later. Good thing too because I was about to walk the fuck up out of there.

"Well, we have your results in. You were the victim of sexual assault. We will give the DNA results to the police department."

"Oh my God! Do I have an STDs?" she asked.

"No, you don't."

"Can I get the Plan B pill?" Tray asked.

"Plan B?" Dr. Lyle asked.

"Uh, so I don't get pregnant by that bastard who raped me!!" she cried.

"I know what the Plan B pill is Trashelle, but it's too late for that."

"What? What do you mean?" Tray asked.

"The tests we ran show that you were already pregnant," Dr. Lyle said.

"What?" we both asked at the same time.

"Are you sure?" Trashelle asked.

"Yes, very sure. Both the urine and blood tests prove positive for pregnancy. So, you see, the Plan B pill isn't an option in this case," Dr. Lyle explained.

I was stunned but wasn't about to get excited or anything. Shit, I didn't know if that baby was mine. With all the niggas that had been all up and through her pussy?

Who knows?!

Chapter Two

Trashelle

Did this doctor just say that I was pregnant? I knew I didn't hear what I thought I heard, but judging by the look on Tyson's face, I heard him right. I was pregnant. How the hell did that shit happen? What the hell was I going to do with a baby? Tyson wasn't even speaking to me. We weren't any closer to getting back together than we were two weeks ago.

"I can't believe that I'm pregnant!" I said in total shock.

"Do you recall when your last menstrual cycle was?"

"Last month, month before last… to be honest doc, I can't remember. My cycle has always been a little irregular," I admitted.

Ever since I got on birth control when I was 17, my cycle had been screwed up. I could have a cycle one month, then none the next. Or sometimes, I'd have one for five days and then one for two days. It was just a sticky situation when it came to my cycle.

"Well, while y'all tryna figure out when the baby is due, how about a paternity test too?" Tyson blurted out embarrassing the hell out of me. I shot him a look so cold that the doctor's face turned beet red. "What?"

Shrugging his shoulders, Tyson continued his rant to the doctor. "I'm serious."

"Well, there's quite a few options..."

"I wanna know how to find out asap!" Tyson insisted with his arms folded across his chest.

"Well, damn!" I huffed and rolled my eyes. I couldn't believe this nigga was really showing out in front of this doctor. Like how embarrassing!

"We ain't even got to go into all the reasons why I'd be asking for this test, do we Tray?! I just wanna know! No, I NEED to know! Doc can you refer us somewhere or something?"

"There's quite a few facilities that can perform the non-invasive procedure that can determine paternity, gender and due date. It's 100% accurate and legal. It only requires for blood to be drawn from the mother and a cheek swab from the father," the doctor explained. "The results are usually available in about a week. But for an additional charge, I believe you can have it rushed in three days or so."

"Yes! That shit right there!" Tyson agreed. "We need to do that this morning..."

"Damn Tyson! Really? I'm haven't even been discharged yet and you tryna drag me to some fucking clinic!"

"Whoa!" the doctor intervened. "I don't mean to interfere, but there's a place in this parking lot and the nurse is already printing up your discharge papers."

Is this muthafucka teaming up with Tyson? Why is he offering all this information when he can clearly see how fucking irritated I was? Ugh! Both of them made me want to cuss them out, but I didn't. Instead, I got my ass up and started getting myself together.

"If y'all gotta discharge me in one of those damn wheelchairs, please get one! I'm ready to go!" I huffed.

"Me too!" Tyson added as the doctor left us alone. "We're going right across the lot and find out what's really going on!"

"We sure the hell are because I ain't going another day hearing your mouth about this shit! I can't believe you're even doubting the paternity Tyson!" I screamed as the nurse came in with my papers and that damn wheelchair.

Refusing to accept the nurse's help, I got my ass up and plopped into the chair myself. Tyson trailed right behind us to the front door.

"Let me go get my truck," he said before disappearing.

"Damn, he's mean!" the nurse whispered. "What's up his ass?"

Yeah, it was unprofessional for her to voice her personal opinion, but in this case, she was dead on the money and I had to agree with her. Tyson was being so evil and very spiteful. I couldn't believe his fucking ass was acting this damn petty.

"He's mad because I cheated on him. Before you stand there and judge me, I always, I mean always, practiced safe sex! That makes me a million percent positive that Tyson is this baby's daddy! Matter of fact, I'll be sure to come up here and show you the proof too! Ain't nobody thinking about him tryna clown somebody! He's gonna be the one looking stupid at the end of that 3rd fucking day! Believe that shit!" I stated surely as Tyson pulled up in his SUV.

Do you know that this fool tried to get his ass out and open the door for me and help me in like he cared about me? After he just clowned me like that? Ugh, I couldn't stand him!

"Thank you so much Nurse Abby. I'll see you soon." I smiled as we drove to the other side of the lot and took those damn tests. I frowned immensely through these damn tests still finding it hard to believe that Tyson was putting me through this.

By the time we were done, I was cussing his damn ass out.

"You know I can't stand yo ass, right?" I grumbled as he drove towards my house.

"I know, but I had to have that shit done before we go any further in this relationship."

"Relationship? We aren't in a damn relationship!" I corrected. I mean, I tried to get back with him, but he didn't want any parts of it. Now, he was talking about a relationship. There wasn't a relationship.

"Well, maybe not, but all I know is I ain't about to be taking care of you and a baby that ain't even mine Tray! I gotta know and you should understand that shit!"

"Okay, let's say I do understand your reasons for wanting to get proof that the baby is yours. Does that mean I'm supposed to let you clown me like you did at that hospital Tyson! That didn't make any sense! You embarrassed the hell outta me and didn't think twice about doing it!"

"I could see how you would feel that way, but that wasn't my intention. So, I do apologize," he said looking over at me with that smile.

Like a dummy, I fell for it and once we got to my place, I invited him in. Tyson helped me in the house, got me in the bed and even made me some hot tea with lemon. He had me feeling special and everything!

Things were all going very well until he went to the bathroom and left his cell on the bed. In that moment, it started ringing. Yes, I answered that shit as soon as I saw Eraina's name pop up on the screen. I mean, why was that chick even calling him if he wasn't still messing around with her?

"What the hell do you want?" I hissed the second the call connected.

"Uh, last time I checked, I was calling Tyson's cell, not yours! Obviously, if I'm calling him, it's because I want to talk to him. But I guess now that I got you on the line bitch, I may as well talk to you! Shit, I've been wanting to have this conversation with you for a while now and you know what? I can't wait to see yo ass! You must've thought I forgot that you pushed me in that fucking nasty ass water, huh?! I see you didn't stick around until I got out because you knew I was gonna beat that ass..."

"I actually didn't think yo' fat ass was gon' make it out the water. I prayed so damn hard that you would sink to the fucking bottom where the rest of your kind is, you bottom feeding bitch!" I shot.

"Who are you talking to?!" Tyson shouted as he came out of the bathroom with a raised brow. "What the fuck? I know damn well you ain't answered my phone Tray!"

"Fuck!" I said, quickly hanging up on Eraina.

I really wished Tyson had given me a couple of more minutes on the phone with her. I regretted that I didn't get the chance to tell that meddling bitch that I was pregnant and about to have a baby by Tyson!

That stupid chick may as well hung up her thoughts on being with my man because after he finds out that the baby I was carrying was his, he will be stuck like Chuck! It didn't matter if it was a boy or girl, this would be his first! Oh, and he wanted kids too?! Yeah, we were about to make our shit official once again!

Ring, ring, ring...

Tyson's cell rang right after, but this time he answered it. It wasn't nobody but Eraina, that bug-a-boo bitch calling back! I was getting tired of her annoying ass already!

"What's up Eraina?" Tyson boldly answered as he walked out of my bedroom to take the call.

Hopping up out of the bed, I ran right on to the doorway so that I could hear what the hell he had to say. I just couldn't understand why he had to take the call privately. What did he need to say that he couldn't have said in front of me? Sneaky muthafucka!

"Nah, I've been busy. What's up?" I heard him say before he paused for a few seconds. After that pause, his tone changed altogether. "Are you fucking kidding me? I'll be there in a minute. Be dressed to go!"

Tyson came back in the room with a stressed look on his face. "I gotta go, but I'll be back."

"Where are you going?" I asked, even though I already knew the answer.

"I got something I gotta handle real quick!"

"You're going to be with her again!"

"Please Tray, don't start. I really got something I need to handle…'

"I won't play second to that bitch Tyson! Not while I'm carrying your baby and not after!" I said trying to make shit clear to him.

"Nobody asked you to, but until that baby is proven to be mine, you can't make no damn demands on me. Like I said before, I got something to do, so I will see you when I get back," he said. "Call me if you need something Tray."

"What I need is for you to stay with me. In case you forgot, I did just get out of the hospital!"

"Call me if you need anything," he repeated before heading out the front door.

Shit, the only fucking thing I needed was for him to come home to me. That was right where he needed to be…

Chapter Three

Eraina

No, that ho' Trashelle did not just answer Tyson's phone like that! I didn't even get to burst her fucking bubble about being pregnant by him, but I sure let him know! That was the only way I got him to agree to come to my house.

When Tyson got here, I was looking good and smelling even better. Handing him my proof of pregnancy and dressing up definitely didn't do the trick because he didn't even look twice at me or the paperwork that I handed him!

Damn. I sure was thinking that I was going to get some! Oh, that was the wrong thing to assume because soon as he stepped into my place, we headed right back out to some paternity testing place.

That was all fine and dandy with me because I knew who the father of my baby was. Obviously, Tyson wasn't so sure.

On the way to the clinic, I must've asked him a dozen questions about the procedure and this nigga had an answer for each one of them. It was like he had already researched the shit before he got to my house. But how could he have done that so fast?

Things got even more peculiar when we stepped inside the medical office and the receptionist addressed Tyson by his name. I immediately asked him did he make us an appointment.

"Yeah, don't trip Eraina. We'll be outta here in no time."

"How do you know so much about all this?"

"Honestly?"

"Yeah, honestly Tyson!"

As this man sat there and told me all about how Trashelle was attacked, I rolled my eyes upward. I needed lightening to strike his ass or something for him to think I gave a damn! That didn't interest me in the least, but what did cause me to do a double take was when Tyson mentioned that Trashelle was pregnant too. I just about died!

"The truth is I had to bring her here earlier for the same damn thing," he admitted like it wasn't a big deal that two women were carrying his baby at the same time!

Shit, it was a big deal to me and the thought of it brought me to tears. I couldn't have held them back if I wanted to and at that moment, I didn't give a damn. My heart was shattered again.

"I really don't know why you're so damn upset. It ain't like you and I were a couple and I cheated on you or anything. If anyone should be upset, it should be me because two women are claiming they're pregnant by me and I can't trust either one of your asses!" Tyson complained as he held on to my hand.

All through the tests he was so supportive and kind. Not mean like he had been lately. It felt so good and made me really believe that we would make a beautiful family, with the baby and all. The more I thought about us having a baby, the more I wanted to be with Tyson. There was no way that I was about to let Trashelle have him! She didn't deserve him one bit!

When she had him, she did nothing but cheat on him time and time again with strangers at that! No, that bitch wasn't about to get him! Tyson was going to be all mine if I had to fight Trashelle every time I saw her ass!

Now I really understood how Nessa could consider doing what Byron asked her to do to his wife! The reason why was because I could already see myself beating that bastard baby out of Trashelle. Nothing but the grace of God could stop me from doing that! Especially after that crazy bitch pushed me in that damn water! I was never going to forget that shit!

"You ready to go?" Tyson asked, snapping me out of my daze as the nurse gave us the rest of our paperwork.

"Yeah, I'm tired after all this. Mentally tired," I complained as we got into his SUV to head back to my apartment.

"You hungry? I can stop by somewhere and get you something before I take you back home."

"Yeah, I am. If you can stop by that pizza place right at the corner, I'd appreciate that. A combination on thin crust would do me just right about now."

"I gotcha," Tyson smiled as he took me right on over there and got me just what I wanted. He even got me a pink lemonade with extra ice just the way I liked!

I didn't know what the hell Tyson was up to, but with the way he was treating me, I wasn't about to complain one bit. With him, no telling how long this special treatment would last, so I planned on milking it as long as I could.

"So, are you coming in?" I asked as he pulled into one of the visitor stalls in my complex's lot.

"You think I'm not about to come in and help you eat that bad boy?" he teased as he got out of the truck and escorted me to the door.

Together, we entered my apartment and tore that pizza up. When it was gone, Tyson got up to leave.

"Look Eraina, these next three days ain't gonna be easy, but hopefully, things will change after these results come back..."

"What does that mean?" I asked with a disappointed look.

"It means that I'm gonna stay in my hotel, but I'll have to check on the both of you. I'm not in a relationship with neither of you, but y'all may both be carrying my seeds. To me, that shit matters. So, bear with me while we figure this shit out, okay Eraina?"

"Okay Tyson," I replied as I stared into his dreamy eyes.

Disappearing out my door, I closed it behind him and ran to call Nessa. I couldn't wait to update her on what was going on!

*****

Those three days seemed to take forever to go by. Why was it that when you were waiting on something, it took forever to get here? Had I not been waiting on those results the days would've been going by so fast.

Don't get me wrong, but I was kind of sad when the day finally came. Only because I was getting used to being taken care of by Tyson. Hopefully, it would continue one he knew for sure that the baby I was carrying was his.

On that third morning, I was on pins and needles waiting for Tyson's call. When it finally came through, I just about passed out.

"What's up?"

"Well, the results just came in..."

"So?"

"So, I found out that you are carrying my baby Eraina and your due date is October 2nd..."

"See! I told you Tyson! I told you that this was your baby! I don't know why you didn't believe me! I told you! I told you!" I repeated happily over and over before I realized that Tyson didn't sound as if he was sharing my joy. "What's wrong? I thought you wanted kids?"

"I did, I mean, I do..."

"What's wrong? Am I that bad of a person to be having a kid by you?" I asked, feeling offended.

"No, I'm not saying that shit at all. It's just that I got Trashelle's results too..."

My stomach dropped. I didn't even want to listen to what was about to come out of Tyson's mouth next because I knew that I would be floored.

"What? What is it Tyson? What did the tests say? Is she pregnant with your baby too? I just know this can't be happening! Tell me Tyson! Just tell me! Is Trashelle having a baby by you too?" I was on tens waiting for him to say something, anything. He was just holding the phone and not saying shit. "Answer me Tyson! Is she carrying your baby?"

"Yes!" he snapped. "She's having my kid..."

"Well, am I at least having my baby first?"

"Actually, you guys are both due on October 2nd..."

"You fucked us on the same day Tyson?!"

"Yeah, but that probably don't have shit to do with it! That shit goes off your last period or something! Y'all was both just probably on your period at the same time or something."

"Nah, you fucked us on the same damn day or close to it!" I cried, feeling like my whole world was crumbling down.

"Why the fuck you tripping for? I used protection with you every time and I still got caught slipping..."

"So, you sorry I'm the one pregnant now?! Is that what you're saying? I guess you only wanted Trashelle to be pregnant huh?!"

"No, I'm saying that I never used protection with her, and I always did with you. What does all that even matter now? I have two women about to have my baby and neither of you are going to get an abortion..."

"Oh, so now you want me to kill our baby Tyson?" I hollered with even more tears spilling from my eyes.

"No! I ain't said no shit like that Eraina and this is just what I don't wanna deal with. Y'all both gonna have to step back and let me figure this shit out. I don't plan on leaving either of you high and dry, but I'm not trying to be with either of you either. I'm good by myself until I can come up with a plan that will work for all three of us."

What Tyson was saying sounded really dumb right now.

"If you're looking for us to be living in the same house on some sister wives bullshit like that show on TV, you can forget that shit!" I said, letting him know if that was what he had in mind, I wasn't down for it.

"Ain't nobody said no shit like that!" he said.

"No, you didn't but I bet you were thinking it!"

"Damn! Can you just give me a fucking minute!"

"Oh, you want a minute? Huh? That's what you want? How about I give you several minutes?!" I asked before I hung the phone up.

Once we hung up, I got to thinking. Instead of fighting with him about his situation, I was about to use my time to get closer to him. While he was taking care of me, I planned on taking care of him even more.

"That bitch is gonna get the short end of the stick whether she wants it or not!" I laughed to myself as I counted down the days until we had to go back to work on the rig. "I may have to share Tyson for his two weeks off, but the two weeks we are out on the water, he's all mine!"

Giggling loudly, I kicked off my slippers and slid into my bed before dialing Nessa up. Preparing myself to listen to her talk shit about me and

Trashelle both being pregnant at the same time by the same nigga, I started in before she could. That shit didn't work too well either...

Chapter Four

Nessa

"I know you fucking lying to me bitch! I know I heard you wrong, so repeat that shit!"

"You heard me right. Me and that bitch are both pregnant by Tyson..."

"What kinda shit is that? I know you ain't still thinking that y'all gon' be together after this shit!" I remarked.

"Why the fuck not? Tyson is happy about our baby..."

"I bet he's just as happy about hers!"

"No, he ain't! He made her take a DNA test to prove the baby was his! You know what that means?"

"Shit, it means the same thing it meant for you bitch! He thinks y'all were both cheating on his ass! The whole time, he's playing both of y'all! Please don't fall for the bullshit Eraina. You're way too smart for that!"

"Things are gonna work out for me and Tyson, just watch!"

"No, bitch, they're not. You really need to just shut up and listen to me!" I screamed out as Eraina kept talking about their plans for after the baby's arrival. I didn't understand how she could be so positive about her situation when Trashelle was pregnant by Tyson too. "This shit is all bad... all of it! Y'all ain't gonna never be rid of that ho'! Even if he does happen to choose you over her, she's always gonna be a factor in his life Eraina! She's gonna have a baby for Tyson to take care of just like you! What the hell is so good about that?"

"I'm having a boy! His first son!" Eraina was sounding so stupid right now. I didn't know if she was trying to convince me or herself that the sex of the baby that she was carrying would have an impact on this situation.

How the hell did she even know she was having a boy if she wasn't due for another seven months? There was no way that test gave her that information. My friend was losing her fucking mind!

This whole thing was fucked all the way up! Why couldn't she see that?

"So, let me ask you something Eraina. How do you know that you're having a boy? And do you think the gender of your baby is going to mean anything when you're both pregnant by the same damn man?"

"Hell yea, it means a lot! And I just know I'm having a boy because I can feel it!"

"You can feel it huh? Please don't say that shit out loud because you sound stupid friend!"

"Excuse you..."

"For real. You sound very dumb. You aren't due for seven months, so how can you possibly say you're having a boy?"

"You know how you can feel something in your gut? I just feel in my gut that I'm having a boy and that bitch is having a girl," she said.

"Yea, you need some serious help. You're not making a lick of sense right now. And just for the record, the gender of your baby isn't gonna matter to Tyson. You wanna know why? Because he's using both you and that other girl..."

"No, he's not!"

"Yes, he is!"

"Well, if he's using me, Byron must be using you!" she countered.

"We're not talking about Byron. We're talking about you, that bitch and Tyson."

"You are such a damn hater!"

"I'm not a hater at all! I don't want you to think that of me when we're best friends. I'm just trying to get you to see that this shit ain't gonna go as smooth as you think it is. Y'all are both pregnant by the same damn man! Take those rose-colored glasses off and see the shit for what it really is Eraina. A HOT ASS MESS!!" I said.

I didn't care if she got mad at me or not, the shit had to be said. She was walking around thinking that because she was having a baby by

Tyson that everything would be all good. That wasn't the case though. Trashelle was pregnant by that nigga too, and I bet the two of them were still fighting over his trifling ass.

"Whatever! You'll see, everything is going to work out for me," she said.

"Damn! It just must be pregnancy season because everyone 'round here getting knocked up but me!" I sighed while lowkey wishing I was pregnant by Byron.

"Girl bye! You don't even need to be pregnant right now, at least not by no married man! I mean, you talking about how Tyson is going back and forth between me and Trashelle, but ain't that the same thing Byron doing with you and his wife? And ain't his wife pregnant too?" Eraina reminded me.

"So! She ain't gonna be pregnant for long," I countered.

"What's that supposed to mean? Please tell me you are not reconsidering doing that foul shit Byron asked you to do. Because if you are, know that you will get caught and I will not be making no weekly, monthly, or yearly visits to the prison to see yo ass! I done told you Nessa!"

"Nobody was saying that, but it's nice to know that you would turn your back on me if I ever got locked up though."

"Don't come at me with that bullshit! If you would land your ass in jail, that would be of your own making, not mine. Not only that, I'm having a baby. I ain't about to be waddling or taking my baby to no prison. Uh, uh, not me!" Eraina clowned. I could imagine her shaking her head right now. "And what's to say you do the deed and get away with it, how do you know that Byron will be with you afterwards?"

"Because he said he would..."

"So what? That man could be telling you anything just to get you to do what he wants you to do! That doesn't guarantee that he'll be with you..."

"Now, who's being a hater?"

"Nope. Not at all. I'm just trying to open your eyes the way you were trying to open mine. Speaking of rose-colored glasses, maybe you should take yours off too BFF. That shit with you, Byron and his wife is much messier than my shit with Tyson. At least Tyson isn't trying to do no foul shit to get us to lose these babies. Think about it," she said. "You could do much better than that lying cheating ass scumbag who wants his own kid dead just so he can be free to do what he wants to do. How could you wanna be with someone like that anyway?"

"I can't help who I love Eraina," I confessed sadly.

"Shit, if who I loved was threatening my damn freedom... never mind. You ain't listening anyway and you're gonna do whatever it is you want to do. Just remember what I said about you getting locked up."

"I'ma talk to you later Eraina," I mumbled with an attitude.

Not bothering to wait for her to respond, I disconnected the call. Eraina had drained me with that damn conversation. How could she think her situation was any different than mine? If anything, hers was worse because another bitch was pregnant by the same man that she wanted to be with... and her ass was pregnant too!

The only person that was pregnant in my case was Byron's wife and he didn't even want that baby. Why was everyone getting pregnant but me? I wanted to have Byron's baby too, but if he was going to try and make me have an accident to lose it, there was no way that was ever going to happen.

There wasn't even a chance that I would get pregnant anytime soon anyhow. Hell, I hadn't even seen Byron in over a week, so I had no idea what he was doing, or he was doing it with. All I knew was that I hadn't been seeing him nor was he answering my calls or text messages.

What if Eraina was right? What if Byron was trying to play me? What if I did help his wife suffer a miscarriage and he turned around and went be with some other bitch? Then what?

I never would've thought that about Byron, but now that I hadn't been seeing him that was all I could think about. I mean, if he loved me so much and wanted me to do that deed so we could be together, where was he? After all that begging me in my face, by phone, and by text to do the shit and he was still not there with me? After I tried to beat that baby out of Regina and he still wasn't here with me? It wasn't my fault that she didn't lose it!

The more I thought about it, the more it made me wonder if Byron had gotten back together with his wife. There was only one way to find that shit out.

Grabbing my purse, cell and keys, I rushed out the door. I now had the address where his wife lived, so of course, I was going there.

"Lord forgive me for the foolishness I'm about to display on these assholes! Lord, because if I find Byron over at that house..." I paused with a deep sigh then continued. "I'ma need you to reach down and touch me Lord because I know that I'ma be mad enough to kill somebody."

The only thing that I could do was pray the whole 30- minute ride to the address. All that came to a cease when low and behold... I turned that corner and there was Byron's car parked in the driveway like it belonged there! That nigga had me waiting on him and thinking that he was living in one of his mama's properties and here he is shacked up over here with his pregnant wife.

"Aw hell naw!" I fumed as I hopped out my car. I popped the trunk and walked to the back.

"This nigga got me fucked up if he thinks he can play me like that!"

Aggressively snatching the tire iron out the back, I walked over to his car. As I stood there with my anger rising, I laid my eyes on his blacked out 2008 Chevy Camaro that he had put his heart, soul, and a whole lot of money into. Lord knows that I couldn't help myself...

BANG! BANG!

Beginning with the back glass, I smashed it out. Stomping around to the driver's side, I continued.

BANG!

Smashed out that window then moved to the front of the car.

BANG!

Next was the front windshield. I only had a chance to hit it once, but it didn't break. By that time, the front door had opened, and Byron was screaming like a little kid.

"WHAT THE FUCK ARE YOU DOING YO?!" he yelled. Ignoring him, I lifted up the tire iron to hit the windshield again. Before I it could connect, he tackled me against the car.

"WHAT THE FUCK ARE YOU DOING HERE BYRON?!! HUH?!!" I hollered in his face.

"BITCH WHAT THE FUCK DID YOU DO TO MY FUCKIN' CAR NESSA?!!" he yelled. He was just as angry as I was, but I didn't care.

My feelings were crushed, and I was tired being a pawn in Byron's fucking game. He was supposed to be mine, but he was still fucking with his wife. That shit had me heated.

It only made me angrier when I looked up and saw that bitch Regina standing at the front door on the phone. She was probably calling the cops on me. I had to get out of here before they carted me off to jail.

"LET ME GO BYRON!! THAT BITCH IS CALLING THE COPS!!" I pled as I stared into his anger filled eyes.

"GOOD! I HOPE THEY COME AND ARREST YOUR ASS!! LOOK WHAT THE FUCK YOU DID TO MY DAMN CAR!!" he continued to shout in my face.

"Byron I'm sorry. I was just so mad when I came over here and saw your car in the driveway," I said in an effort to calm him down and get him to let me go.

"I DON'T GIVE A FUCK WHY YOU DID IT BITCH!! LOOK AT MY FUCKING CAR NESSA!!"

All this nigga was worried about was his car, while I was worried about being arrested. His wife had ended the call and was standing there with her arms across her chest and a smirk on her face.

"WHAT THE FUCK YOU SMILING AT BITCH?!!" I asked angrily.

"I'm not smiling. I'm laughing at your dumb ass! You did all this just to end up in jail behind a man who doesn't even want your pathetic, pitiful, dumb ass!" Regina taunted.

"LET ME GO BYRON!!" I cried as I struggled to break free. "Just let me smack her ass one good time!"

"I ain't letting you go for shit! Not til the police get here!"

Oh damn! That bitch was seriously trying to get me locked up. If that was true and the police were coming, I was going to give them a real good reason to arrest me if I could just get Byron to turn me loose!

He wouldn't have to worry about her having a miscarriage because I was going to kill that bitch! Never in my life had I wanted someone dead the way I did right now.

"Oh, hell no!" I mumbled as I listened to the sirens approaching. Now I was desperate to be let go. "Please let me go Byron! I don't wanna go to jail!" I begged.

"YOU SHOULD'VE THOUGHT ABOUT THAT SHIT BEFORE YOU CAME HERE AND FUCKED UP MY DAMN CAR NESSA!!"

"If you loved me, you'd let me go!"

"LOOK AT MY FUCKIN' CAR BITCH!!" he yelled as spittle flew in my face.

I couldn't believe that was the only thing he was thinking about. I mean, I knew I was wrong for fucking up his car, but he pissed me off. Knowing how much he loved it was the deciding factor when I busted out his windows. But I never expected him to let me get arrested. I thought he'd be mad with me, but then he'd come by later and we'd laugh about how crazy I was.

I just figured he'd tell me to fix his car and that would be it. Never had I imagined it going like this.

"Is that all you're worried about? Your fucking car? What about me Byron? Don't you care about me and how I feel?" I asked as tears streamed from my eyes.

"NO BITCH! HE DOESN'T GIVE A SHIT ABOUT YOUR DUMB ASS!!" Regina replied. "Tell her Byron..."

"Regina, go in the fucking house please!"

"No! Not until you tell that bitch how much she doesn't mean to you!" Regina continued. "Tell her that she ain't the only bitch you been fucking!!"

What the fuck was that bitch talking about? What did she mean by saying I wasn't the only bitch Byron been fucking? Who the hell else was this man, who claimed to love me, sleeping with?

"WHAT THE HELL IS SHE TALKING ABOUT BYRON?!!" I asked as I looked into his eyes.

The police cruiser pulled into the driveway and the cop got out and approached us. He took one look at the car and let out a low whistle. "Damn! This was a really nice ride!"

"Ya think?" Byron asked while still holding on to me. "Here!" He thrust me toward the cop angrily. "Arrest her for fucking up my car!"

"What?" I asked, begging him with my eyes. "Byron are you serious right now, babe!"

"Don't even try that shit with me Nessa! You damn right I'm serious! Arrest that bitch for destroying my fucking property!" Byron said with a mean scowl on his face as he grimaced at me. The look on his face had me thinking I stunk or something.

The way he was scowling at me you would think I smelled like shit or something worse.

"Ma'am I am placing you under arrest for the destruction of property and disturbing the peace."

"What? Are you serious?"

"Yes ma'am. You have the right to remain silent..."

"Byron! Byron fa real!"

"If you give up that right to remain silent, anything you say can and will be used against you in a court of law..."

"After everything we've been through Byron... you gon' do me like this for real?"

"You have the right to an attorney. If you cannot afford one, the courts will appoint one for you. Do you understand your rights as I have read them to you ma'am?"

"Byron please do something! I'm sorry!" I pled for him to not go through with this.

If he was trying to scare me, it worked. I was scared as fuck about going to jail. If he wanted to teach me a lesson, I got it loud and clear.

Don't fuck with his property.

"Get that bitch off my damn property!" Byron said.

The cop tugged on my arm as I busted out in full blown crying mode. I didn't give two shits if the whole neighborhood was watching right now. I didn't want to go to jail and I'd do anything to keep that from happening. Tears streamed down my face as I realized Byron wasn't going to do a damn thing to help me.

The cop ushered me into the back seat of his patrol car as Byron stood there with his hands- on top of his head looking at his car. He really cared more about that fucking vehicle than he did me. His wife was still standing on their front porch with a huge grin on her face. She seemed to be the only one taking pleasure out of seeing this whole situation. But I had something for her... for both of them!

Don't believe me, just watch!

Chapter Five

Byron

This shit was ridiculous. The nerve of Nessa! To come to my wife's fucking house and act a fool like that? Fuck my car up like that? And she didn't think that her ass was going to go to jail! Yeah, a nigga was mad heated about that shit. She had me fucked up if she thought she was going to get away with that shit.

"What the fuck was that?" Regina asked once we had gone inside the house.

"What are you talking about?" I asked. I was already irritated and aggravated, so she would want to go play in traffic or something. It would be much safer than playing with me right now.

"I mean, that bitch coming over here! How the hell did she even know where I live Byron?!"

"Fuck, I'on know! What the fuck you asking me that shit for?"

"Cuz she's your bitch! She should be your fuckin' problem, not mine!" Regina said.

"She is my fuckin' problem! Did you or did you not just see what she did to my fuckin' car?!!" I asked.

"She's my problem too because she brought that shit to my fucking house! I'm pregnant Byron!

How do you think this damn stress is affecting the baby?"

I didn't give two fucks about her or that damn baby! The only reason I was here was to check on her ass and look what the fuck happened.

"Well, maybe she found you the same way you found her! How the hell you know where she lived Regina?! Did you follow me over there?!"

"Stupid! Your Chevy has OnStar and I have the damn app on my cell too! It tells all your trips and the details including the address and how long you were at your destination! After checking your history, I learned a whole lot!"

"Well, obviously you didn't learn how to shut the hell up and mind your own damn business! We're separated Regina!" I spat. "Why the fuck you mad anyway?! I'm the one who should be mad! My fucking car is completely destroyed!"

"That's what the hell you get for cheating on me!" Regina snapped while rolling her neck.

Giving her a look that could kill, I shook my head and thought about walking right back out that door. The only thing that stopped me was her calming her ass down and apologizing.

"Why were you seeing her anyway? I definitely don't know what you saw in her except that big ass and those fake titties!" my wife hated.

"Her tits aren't fake," I said with a smile.

I knew that shit would get under her skin. I didn't care though because like I said, I was irritated.

"If you're gonna keep talking about her, I'm gonna go ahead and get up outta here. I really don't feel like hearing all that shit Regina."

"Oh, so you're gonna leave?"

"Yeah, just call me if you need something."

"I need you to be here for me... for us! For me and the baby Byron!" Regina nagged getting on my nerves even more. Damn, I wished she lived on the second- floor so I could push her down the stairs myself just to get her to close her mouth.

Unfortunately, I couldn't even if I wanted to. Regina was my wife and she was carrying my seed for sure. I didn't like it, but what could I do about it?

"WE ARE NOT FINISHED WITH THIS CONVERSATION!!"

"I am," I said as I headed for the front door.

"COME BACK HERE BYRON!!" she yelled as she followed right behind me. She grabbed my arm and tried to turn me around.

"Don't put your hands on me Regina! I done sent one bitch to jail today, don't make it two!" I threatened.

That must've been the wrong thing to say because before I could get ahold of the knob to close the door behind me, this crazy woman hit me with a set of marbled coasters. It didn't knock me out, but it drew blood.

"Oh, so you do wanna go to jail?!" I grunted ready to ring her neck.

Before I could make a move, Regina slammed the door on me and double bolted it from the inside. This security feature prevented me from getting in there and putting hands on her and that was a good thing. If I did that shit, I would be the one getting locked up next.

"Good luck with getting home!" Regina yelled out through the front window.

Looking at my car, I immediately remembered that I didn't have a way home! Now I was stuck looking stupid.

"Fuck!"

Instead of standing there risking more drama to jump off, I got a Lyft to pick me up down the street at HEB. Walking over there, I dialed up my insurance company.

Thankfully they said that they would be able to take care of everything, including towing it to a nearby repair shop. Now that I was able to breathe a little better, I was cool. Well, all except for the damn headache I had from Regina hitting me with those damn coasters.

Once I wrapped up the insurance call, Regina's calls started blaring. I had been ignoring them while on the phone and I continued to do so. Shit, this was Regina's tenth time calling me. After that, I blocked her number altogether and slid my phone down in my back pants pocket.

"Byron?" the young guy driving the black Altima called out as I strolled into the parking lot of HEB.

"Yeah."

Climbing into the backseat, I headed straight home to shower and tend to my wound. After I finished and slipped on some sweats and a T-shirt, I called my job up. I needed to take a day off to get a rental and get my head together.

"Let me pour a damn drink and try to relax," I mumbled to myself as I grabbed a glass from the kitchen cabinet.

Popping the top off a fresh fifth of Crown, I poured a double. With the drink in hand, I went to chill in my bedroom. Snatching up the remote control off the nightstand after setting my glass down, I turned on the 50- inch TV that I had mounted on the far wall and tuned in to BET.

"Ain't shit on," I huffed as my cell began to ring. Getting up off my bed, I went in the bathroom after I realized I had left my phone on the counter. "How the hell she get out so fucking fast?"

Debating whether or not I should answer it, I messed around and missed it. Nessa was the last person I wanted to talk to after the stunt she pulled.

Ring, ring, ring...

The chick wasn't letting up and I was curious as hell how she got out of jail already, so after Nessa's third attempt, I finally answered. That made me regret sliding that green phone icon right away.

"Nigga I hope you know that you done fucked up now!"

"How the hell they let you out so soon?"

Ding, ding, ding...

As I was questioning Nessa, a series of familiar alerts sounded off. They were text messages.

"You may wanna check them texts Byron!"

Drawing my cell from my ear, I read three messages that I had sent Nessa about making Regina lose her baby! This bitch was crazy!

"Didn't you tell me that you deleted all that shit Nessa?!"

"I did, but I screenshot all of it before I erased them Byron! I'm glad I did after you got me locked up like that in front of your wife!" she screamed at the top of her lungs. "And if you think that's bad, I got those two voicemails you left me too!"

"You wouldn't Nessa!" I began to panic.

"Meet me at my apartment in an hour! Eraina is on her way to get me and she's dropping me off."

"I ain't coming over there..."

"I'm still at the station and I can release all this shit to them right the fuck now and get a case started against you Byron! Y'all probably already done had the cops come to your house before as crazy as y'all are!" Nessa clowned. "Better yet, why don't I send all these to Regina? I'm sure with this proof she'll believe me and probably go to the cops herself!"

"You ain't gotta do all that!" I huffed giving in. "I'll be there in an hour Nessa and don't do no stupid shit!"

"Be at my place and you won't have to worry about all that!" she spat with her slick tongue before she hung up on me.

Yeah, Nessa may have had the upper hand, but I had something for her ass. I was about to go over there and fuck the daylights out of her if I had to in order to get her cell and smash it to pieces. That way she couldn't hold shit over my head.

Thinking I had things all figured out, I got outside and remembered that I didn't have my damn car. Now my dumb ass was stuck to catch a damn Lyft round trip because I definitely didn't plan on staying the night or having Nessa pick me up.

Getting on my app once again, I had a car pick me up and take me over there. I even paid him $50 extra to pick me back up at midnight. That gave me plenty of time to take care of my business.

When I arrived at Nessa's about an hour later, her homegirl Eraina was just dropping her off. That snobby bitch had the nerve to shoot me a dirty look before she tore off around the corner. I started to kick her ride, but she took off too fast.

"Right on time huh?" Nessa tried to clown as we walked to her door.

"What do you want from me?" I asked trying to get to the point.

"First, I wanna apologize again for messing up your car. I'll pay the deductible, but you gotta drop those charges Byron."

"Yeah, as long as you pay that deductible, we cool Nessa," I lied. She had me fucked up if she thought that I was forgiving her for that shit!

"I gotta take a shower right quick. Being in that funky ass jail made me itch from the top of my head to my ass crack!" she complained. "I'll be right back unless you wanna join me..."

"Have a drink with me first. I know you got some of that Crown in there," I suggested, ready to get Nessa tipsy.

"Okay, I do need something to help me unwind."

Sitting in her kitchen for the next hour or so, we shot the shit and got more than tipsy. I got a little carried away and had to slow my ass down before I fucked up the plan.

"Come on, let's get in the shower baby," Nessa wooed as she rubbed on my manhood. That was all it took for me to strip and join her under the warm streams of water.

Inside, she blessed me with some bomb ass head, but then made the mistake of thinking that I was about to go up in her raw. I was drunk, but I wasn't that damn drunk!

"Come on Byron! Why are you trippin'?" Nessa slurred as she pulled me to her bed while both of our bodies were still dripping wet.

"Because I ain't tryna knock you up baby," I mumbled as I began to push her back a bit, but she was right back on me!

Nessa started to compare us and our relationship to her friend Eraina's situation, and ours was nothing like that. I didn't know who the hell this Tyson nigga was, but I wasn't down for having two chicks pregnant by me at the same time!

No buddy!

Finally, after a couple of minutes, I was able to convince Nessa to let me put on a condom. Once equipped, I tore that ass up just like I planned and by a quarter to 12, I was washing up and she was snoring.

By midnight, I was dressed, and Nessa's cell was floating in the toilet. By the time she would find it, I was sure that it would be fried.

Hurrying out the door as quiet as possible, I went outside to meet the Lyft driver that was waiting for me. Jumping in and getting comfortable in the back seat, I waited for him to drive me home.

As soon as he dropped me off, I went inside my place and jumped in the bed. I fell right to sleep and slept through the night like a newborn baby.

I slept so good that I didn't wake up until after 7am. That was when I got a call from an unknown number.

Thinking that it could have been from my job, I answered it only to hear Nessa screaming in my ear about ruining her phone. I wanted to laugh, but when she enlightened me that everything was saved to the 'cloud', I could've just kicked myself.

How could I be that damn stupid?

Chapter Six

Tyson

The shocking news of having not one, but two kids around the same damn time still had me tripping. I went from wanting a baby to having two by two different women. What the hell was I thinking?

Ready to relieve some stress, I decided to hit the gym with one of my co-workers, Johnson. He lived in Houston too and worked the same rotation on the rig as I did.

"What's good Tyson?" he greeted as he met me by the mats.

"Nigga! You wouldn't believe what I've been going through!"

"I can only imagine after I heard about your girl pushing Eraina in the water!" he clowned.

"That ain't shit!" I added as I explained that both of them were pregnant by me and had the same damn due date.

"Nigga you're kidding!" he expressed as he stared at me.

"Does it look like I'm kidding?" I asked with a straight line across my face.

"Aye, kids are a blessing. Just be happy and enjoy this shit before the babies come Tyson! You basically got a free pass to fuck two different women for the next several months!"

This fool was talking nonsense! Getting pussy was the least of my concerns.

"Nigga, getting pussy by the two of them is what got me in this situation in the first place!"

"No, getting pussy without a condom is what got you in that situation!" he corrected.

"Whatever! I didn't ask you to come down here to teach me some kind of life lesson Johnson. I asked you down here so we could have a talk about what the fuck I should do! I got two chicks pregnant by me and they're both driving me crazy man!"

"I can't imagine what you going through bro, but you should've thought about that before you decided to stick it to both of them. I mean, you said you and Eraina wasn't even on the level that you used to be with Trashelle, so I can't imagine why you wouldn't use a condom with her ass. Are you sure you were the only one she was fucking?"

"Shit don't think I ain't wondered that shit myself man! I was actually praying that she had been fucking with some other nigga, but we took a test and I'm the daddy," I said.

"Wow! So, I guess it ain't gon' do no good to deny that shit until she gives birth then huh?" he said with a laugh.

"No shit Sherlock!" I smirked.

"I don't know what to tell you bro. Where do things stand with you and Trashelle? Are y'all getting back together?" Johnson asked.

"Hell no! I can't trust her ass! She was out there fucking other niggas and shit while I was offshore working to pay the bills in the house! I can't take her back after that shit!"

I didn't tell Johnson everything about that situation. I mean, he knew that Trashelle cheated on me, but he didn't know she was out there fucking niggas for money. I couldn't put her out there like that as my baby mama. Not only would that fuck up her image, but it would make me look bad too. I mean, what kind of nigga tried to wife a bitch who had niggas paying for her pussy?

Not a bitch that I'd want to marry for sure. Unfortunately, Trashelle and I were going to be tied to each other for a lifetime because we were going to be co-parents. I wasn't trying to get back together with her even though I knew she was hoping that I would. I just couldn't do it. I couldn't get back with her when I knew what she was doing.

"Yea, I don't blame you bruh. If my ol' lady had cheated on me, I don't think I'd be able to forgive that shit either..."

"I mean, I forgave her. I just can't be with her."

I wasn't lying about forgiving Tray because I had. I just couldn't forget what she did, so there was no way that I'd be with her like that again. She was going to have to live with that shit and just learn to deal with the new relationship we had. There was no going back to the way things used to be or nothing like that because I wasn't interested in her like that no more.

It kind of felt weird though. We spoke about her having a baby before all that shit happened. I told her that I couldn't wait to be a dad and her husband. Now, look at us. Living in two different places and barely speaking yet still about to share a child.

"So, are you still gonna keep living in the hotel?" Johnson asked bringing my attention back towards him.

"Nah, I can't do that shit no more. I went house hunting before all this shit and found one that I liked. I contacted the realtor and put in an offer, so I should be finalizing and closing the deal by the end of the week. I can't be raising no baby in no hotel room," I explained.

"Good for you man! I'm happy for you!" Johnson replied as he shook my hand.

"Thanks man. Closing this deal will be good and bad..."

"Whatchu mean?"

"Well, it'll be a good thing because I'll have my own crib and shit. But it'll be a bad thing because I was trying to holla at the agent, but she said she didn't wanna mix business with pleasure."

"I could understand that."

"Yea, me too. I understood and respected it."

"But the deal is about to be done, so you gonna ask her out?" he asked.

"Nah, can't do it now."

"What? Why not?"

"Really bro? With all the shit I just told you about these two baby mamas, you think I'm about to add someone else to the mix?" I questioned him with a raised brow and added a smirk.

"Aye, I'd still ask her."

"But what about those two fools I done knocked up? I couldn't start out fresh without exposing that shit! I would need to tell her that I'm expecting two babies!"

"Not unless y'all hit it off further than that first date. If you take her on the first date and she really likes you and you really like her, then mention to her that you have two baby mamas that are pregnant."

"I don't know man. That shit sounds like a disaster waiting to happen. I might like that girl more than I already do. Then when I break the news to her, that'll be it for us."

"Maybe not man. Shit, if she's mature, she may just say fuck what you told her and try to ride out with you anyway," he reasoned.

"I don't know. I may tell her about it before asking her out."

"Well, you can kiss that shit goodbye if you plan on doing that Tyson!" he said as he threw his head back and laughed.

"See! It makes no sense to ask her out then," I said.

"She may understand..."

"Now, you know damn well she ain't finna understand shit! It looks like I was cheating on one of the women when I really wasn't. I'll just have to let that shit go," I said.

"So, you might as well get back together with Trashelle or see if you can work things out with Eraina..."

"Now you trippin'!" I grunted and shook my head.

"I mean, if you ain't gonna try to make it with anyone else because they won't accept your two baby mamas, you may as well try to make shit work with one of them," he explained.

"Nothing about that shit yo ass is saying sounds like it would work Johnson, but I do see what you're saying."

"Good. I think you should go for it with the agent," Johnson pushed again making me agree.

"Maybe I will."

****

That one workout had a nigga sore from head to toe. I even stayed home a couple of more days only to be constantly harassed by Tray and Eraina. I didn't entertain any of their attempts to reach me by refraining from answering calls, texts or my damn door! Honestly, I hadn't even had enough energy or lift to do a damn thing until the realtor Tanya Shaw contacted me with good news.

The deal for the house had gone through and she wanted to meet me there to sign the papers. I told her I could meet her in an hour, took a quick shower and headed there.

When I arrived, I noticed right away that Tanya looked just as beautiful as the last time I saw her. As I stared at her, I remembered what Johnson said about taking her out first, but I didn't feel right about that. It made me feel like I was deceiving her or something and I didn't want that shit on my chest.

"Congratulations on your new home!" Tanya sang out as we neared each other.

Using a hug to greet, we broke the hold and Tanya got right down to business as we entered the house. Setting all the documents on the white marbled top counters, she handed me an ink pen with a smile.

Jotting down my name on the highlighted areas and initialing all the appropriate boxes, I bit down on my bottom lip and smiled again feeling truly proud of myself.

"Here you go," I hummed as I passed her the ink pen back before she congratulated me and hugged me again.

"I couldn't have done this without you," I acknowledged.

"Sure, you could've. All you needed was a dedicated agent," she sang with a wink. "Any one of us could've done it."

"Well, I'm glad I chose you Tanya. You seemed to be the perfect pick!" I whispered bravely before I pulled her close to me.

"Tyson..."

"What? You said no mixing pleasure with business. We're done with the business," I reminded.

"I know but..."

Pressing my lips up against her in hopes of silencing her, I enjoyed the softness and fresh minty taste. Tanya didn't resist even a little, so that gave me the green light to make the kiss last a bit longer.

Tanya moaned as I pulled her closer while stroking her back gently. After we tongue kissed for several minutes, she finally pushed me back. Immediately, I began to stare into her eyes to try to read her.

As they fluttered, she placed her hand on my chest and sighed heavily like she was trying to catch her breath. "Whew!"

Before I could respond, my phone started ringing. I pulled it from my pocket and checked the screen. When I saw that it was Eraina calling me, I hit the vibrate mode then shoved my cell back in my pocket.

"You're not going to get that?" Tanya asked.

"Nope."

"Why not?"

"Because it ain't important," I replied.

"Tell that to the person who keeps calling you," she said as my phone started to ring again.

"It's cool..."

"You know what Tyson? I think that kiss was a mistake and we should just end things right here, right now! I am not into dudes who got stuff to hide!"

"What? Who says I'm hiding anything?"

Tanya stared at me sideways before responding. "You must think I'm stupid huh?"

"Never that."

"You must think something like that! I can clearly see you're hiding something..."

"I was trying not to have to go there," I said as I ran my hand down my face.

"Go where?" she asked.

"Look Tanya, I like you. I like you a lot, actually. But the truth is my exes are pregnant..."

"Exes? As in more than one?"

"Yea, as in two."

"Oh wow! So, you were having sex with both women at the same time?"

"No, definitely not at the same time!"

"But within the same timeframe!" Tanya gasped.

"It's not like that. I was dating this girl, but we broke up. Then I started messing around with another chick and we just fell off. Now, they're both pregnant," I explained.

"Yea, that sounds like a little too much for me. Look Tyson, you're a really nice guy and I thought we could've gotten to know each other better once the sale was complete and our business was done. But to be honest, I'm not looking to go into a relationship with someone who has that much baggage. This is all too much," she explained with a sad expression.

"I understand. I wish you would look pass all that irrelevant shit though..."

"Irrelevant?" she asked with a questioning gaze. "Your phone has been ringing nonstop for the past ten minutes. That lets me know that there will be issues once your kids are born. I'm not with it. I'm sorry."

"Don't apologize. It's cool."

"Take care of yourself. Enjoy the house," she said before she rushed out the door.

Damn! I should've listened to Johnson!

Chapter Seven

Trashelle

For the past two days, the weather here in Houston had been ugly. From heavy rain and winds to sudden power outages.

Drawing the blinds back, I glared out into the night as the bolts of lightning lit up the sky. The sound of thunder was right behind it each time and the loud noises had me jumping out of my skin. I hated loud noises like that especially when I had no one next to me to comfort me.

"Ugh! I hate being here by my damn self!" I complained as I spun around and reflected on where I was a month ago and where I was now.

It was crazy how I went from spending several nights a week with different men for money, to being all alone with limited funds, at home with a baby on the way. It was even crazier how Tyson had wanted so badly for me to have his baby and now that I was having it, he was nowhere to be found! Yeah, knocked up by a nigga that didn't give a fuck! Shit, he was probably over there with Eraina right now!

"Why that nigga ain't even tried to call and check on me?! Jose could still be out there trying to get me and where is Tyson?! I could be laying up in here dead and no one would even know! Damn, I am carrying his baby!"

With sadness creeping through my body, tears began to stream down my cheeks. Jealously as well as envy was added once I started meditating on how Eraina was about to be with Tyson and I wouldn't be anywhere around to stop it. Ugh!

"That miserable bitch!" I grunted as I thought of my man with that big butch looking bitch.

As tall and thick as Eraina was, then the way I always saw her dressed at the docks in those coveralls was the main reason I believed her when she said she was a lesbian. My dumb ass fell right for it too... like a damn fool!

All the while, Eraina was fucking Tyson!

Those two had my nerves wrecked and I was about to drive myself crazy worrying about them being together for the next two weeks.

Tyson's crew was scheduled to leave for their hitch in less than a week. That was how much time I had to try to get him to remember why he fell in love with me in the first place. Otherwise, I risked losing him altogether.

"I wonder if that bitch knows I'm pregnant," I pondered. "Shit if she doesn't, she about to find out!" I sat there thinking of a way to make sure she did. Maybe that would scare the ugly manly looking bitch away!

Since all that mess happened on social media with Eraina before, I had deactivated all my accounts, but now it was time to get right back on there and make a few things clear. I didn't care how petty and childish it made me look. I was ready to wreak some serious havoc when it came to securing the relationship I had with my baby daddy. Tyson was about to get back on the right page and be here with me and his child that I was carrying if I had anything to say about it!

"I already proved my baby is his! Damn! What more does he want from me?"

Huffing heavily, I sat down in front of the desktop in the family room off the kitchen. Soon as I lifted my cell up to set it on the small oak desk, it started ringing just as the claps from the thunder shook my whole place.

Fumbling with my phone, I was finally able to answer the call from my cousin Cina. The moment we were connected all I heard was her blabbing some shit out of control. It sounded like a bunch of jibber jabber and I couldn't understand a word that she was trying to say.

"What the hell are you saying Cina?" I asked calmly and waited for to tell me.

"Have you been on social media...?"

"Which one?"

"Hell, any of them! I mean Snap, Facebook and fucking Instagram..."

"No why? What's going on?"

Suddenly the lights flickered and there were two loud booms. Damn if I didn't almost fall out of the chair when I tried to duck and lean! Quickly getting myself back together, I drew my attention back to the phone conversation with my cousin.

"What's on social media Cina?" I questioned in between the thunder and lightning performance that was going on outside.

"Some chick is tagging you in a bunch of shit..."

Beep, beep, beep... battery critically low... beep, beep, beep...

My cell was quickly dying, and my headset was already dead. "Fuck!"

"Did you hear me Trashelle?!" Cina yelled out into the phone.

"I was trying to but my freakin' phone is dying! I'm trying to find the damn charger Cina! Hold on!" I said as I hopped up from the small desk and ran to my room to get the charger.

Before I could make it to my bedroom, the battery died in my phone and the lights began to flicker again. "Not now Lord! Please don't leave me sitting in the dark!" I begged snatching the charger from the wall before darting back into the family room.

Plopping down in the computer chair, I leaned to plug my cell in. After checking the connection, I tried to power it on a couple of times then quickly discovered that it didn't have enough juice to come on.

Setting my cell down on the desk in defeat, I sat back in the chair and swirled it to face the computer screen just as there was another booming sound outside. This time the noise was even louder. So much so, that I nearly pissed in my damn shorts!

"Damn!" I screamed as all my lights went off, including the one on my computer! "This is not happening right now!"

The silence inside my home allowed me to hear all the eerie noises going on outside. There was whistling, howling and a bunch of pounding like someone was trying to get inside my house.

Trembling all over, I stood up to run to my room to hide, but my legs wouldn't move. Idling in one spot for the next couple of minutes, I didn't budge until the power popped back on.

"Thank you, Jesus!" I chanted nervously as I sat back down at the computer and made sure my cell was charging. "Really? Just one fucking percent?!"

Shaking my head, I turned my computer back on and waited for it to boot up. I was anxious to get on Facebook or Instagram and find out who the hell was tagging me in shit. My cell prevented me from calling or checking my social media timelines and that shit was making me more frustrated.

"Yes!" I whispered as I pulled up Facebook and hurried up to log on.

Pushing the notification icon as soon as my page pulled up, the fucking lights went off again! Boy was my bad luck flowing! The shit was really pissing me off big time.

Standing back up again in the dark, I felt my way to the kitchen to grab the lighter and candles out of the top drawer closest to the back door. Once I got everything out, there was a series of bangs at the back door.

"Fuck!" I screamed and hollered as Jose's face popped up in the kitchen window at the same time another lightning bolt struck. "You better get the fuck away from here Jose! The police are coming!" I bluffed hoping that fool would get off my property.

"Bitch I told you I would be back. I'm gonna kill you tonight... believe that! If I can't have you, no one else will either!"

"Why are you doing this to me?!" I cried pulling out the second drawer nearest to me trying to find a weapon. Instead, I found something better!

Drawing out an old cell phone that had just enough power to turn on, I dialed 911 and threatened him. Jose didn't give a damn. He was still talking shit until something, or should I say someone scared him off.

"You better get from 'round here boy before I put a couple of bullets in your ass!" I heard someone say.

As Jose's face disappeared into the darkness, I heard a couple of gunshots pop off before my neighbor appeared in the window.

"Are you okay baby?" the older black woman asked as she checked behind her.

"Yeah! Did you kill him?!" I panicked.

"No, that bastard got away! I already hear the police coming. Let me go meet them out front and let them know it was me that was shooting."

Looking closely, I could see the blood seeping through her blue terry robe. "Are you okay?" I asked finally opening the back door.

"Yeah, it's nothing. I just got caught on something trying to make my way over here! You stay locked inside and I'll have the cops come to the front door after they're done securing the area and questioning me," she explained before walking around to the front.

As I turned around, the lights popped on again. Now with the hallway lit, I rushed back to my computer and cell. I needed whichever was going to come on the fastest.

"Come on now!" I chanted anxious to call Tyson and let him know what was going on. I didn't give a shit about nothing else! Right now, I needed to talk to him!

Reaching over to check my cell, I found it at a measly five percent, but it was enough to power on and make a call. Too fucking bad Tyson wasn't answering me. In fact, I think he had my darn number blocked!

Now a bitch was heated to say the least and all I could do was try to figure out a way to get in touch with him. How the hell could he have me blocked? I was the mother of his child and I needed to be able to contact him! Didn't he even consider that I might have an emergency or something? That was very selfish of Tyson and so unlike him!

Fuck that computer, social media or whatever else was going on! I needed my man! I needed Tyson!

And he betta not be with that bitch Eraina!

Chapter Eight

Eraina

For the past few days, Tyson had been ignoring me. He even went so far as to block my number. I couldn't even reach him from another number. I was starting to think he had changed his number altogether, but wouldn't it say the line was disconnected? I was so confused at this point.

As his baby mama, you would think that he would have an open line of communication between us. What if there was an emergency and I needed help? How the hell was I going to reach him if I couldn't call him.

Being desperate, I had even called the hotel that he was staying at. When the receptionist answered, I asked for his room but found out that he had moved from there. Now I didn't know where he was.

"We're both pregnant! Ugh! I need him too! Tyson betta choose or split our time equal, or something, shit!" I huffed and thought about Trashelle. "Yeah, I know she's knocked up, but I bet... I bet that bitch don't know that I am too! I bet that shit!"

Feeling discouraged and pissed that Tyson was doing me so wrong, I got desperate and began posting shit on Facebook and Instagram about being pregnant. Trashelle needed to know and be just as hurt as I was! She needed to know that she wasn't the only one that was having Tyson's first kid!

"Ugh, and now look! This girl's page ain't pulling up!"

After seeing that Trashelle had deactivated her accounts, I got bold and tagged her and a bunch of her friends hoping to get some type of reaction from anyone, but nothing.

That bitch needed to know everything! Oh! I couldn't wait for that snooty ho' to find out! She would surely shit in her fucking pants!

Laughing to myself as I climbed out of my bed, I went to the kitchen to get a snack while I called Nessa to see what she was up to.

"Hey boo!"

"I was just about to call yo' ass..."

"Why? What did I do?"

"I'm just now seeing all them damn posts about how you are about to have a baby! You even posted your paperwork telling all your fucking business! Girl, you crazy Eraina!"

"I had to do something to let that bitch Trashelle know that I wasn't going anywhere! I don't know if she knows that I'm pregnant, but if she didn't know, her ass knows now!" I convinced.

"Right, but what do you think Tyson will say when he finds out you did that shit?"

"What you mean?"

"I mean, if he didn't have a conversation with her about you being pregnant and she finds out on social media, don't you think that will piss him off? I thought your goal was to make him come back to you..."

"Well, yea!"

"Then you're going about it all wrong cuz," Nessa enlightened.

"What would you know about it, Nessa? Aren't you still going at it with Byron and Regina?"

"Hell no! I'm done with both them bitches!" she said. "That nigga actually pressed charges on me, girl for damaging his whip! Can you believe that shit?"

"Hell yea, I can believe it! You took a tire iron to that nigga's car! What did you think was gonna happen?"

"I knew he would be mad, but I didn't think he'd be mad enough to have the cops arrest me. Like what kinda shit is that? This whole time, he had been telling me how much he couldn't stand his wife and I was believing him. Something told me to go ride by her house and check to see if he was there. When I saw his car in the driveway, I just lost it!"

"Oh, trust me, I understand. I'm just saying that you can't really give me advice on what not to do when you out there wilin' too cuz!" I said as we both laughed.

"I guess, but you out there advertising your pregnancy on social media ain't cool. At least remove the paperwork with all your business on it."

"Okay, I'll whiten some of the info out, but my name is staying up there. I want that bitch to know that she ain't the only one carrying Tyson's baby!"

"It just seems crazy for y'all to continue beefing for a dude who cheated on both of y'all with no problem. I mean, you deserve better cuz," Nessa said.

"Shit, so do you!"

"Exactly, and that's why I decided to let Byron alone. The shit he's trying to do to his wife can come back to haunt me. It just ain't worth it to me. I am way too cute to spend any more time behind bars!" Nessa stated. "It's bitches in there just waiting to turn me out. No thank you!"

"So, what are you saying? That I should give up on Tyson? Because I ain't ready to do that just yet," I said. "I mean, it would be easier to walk away from him if I wasn't carrying his baby, but I am. Not just that, but I fell in love with his ass!"

"I love Byron too, but I love myself more. While he was holding me down for the police to come arrest me, do you know what that bitch was doing?"

"Yea, laughing at you! You already told me that, remember?"

"Yea, she was laughing at me. That's some crazy shit! Like, she knows her man and I were sleeping together, but she still wants to stay with him. Either she's stupid as fuck or just desperate," Nessa continued.

"Maybe she's not stupid or desperate. Maybe she's just in love with him. Or maybe like me, she just wants to give her child a family," I reasoned.

"That nigga is trying to kill her!"

"But she doesn't know that shit!" I argued.

"Maybe she should know," Nessa said.

"Bitch don't you dare! If you go mouthing off and saying some shit to her, that will put you in the line of fire."

"What do you mean?"

"The police will ask you how you know that. What are you going to tell them? That you were plotting to do what he asked you to do?"

"Hell no! That would be dumb!" Thunder boomed outside causing both of us to let out sharp screams. "Ugh! I hate this fucking weather!"

"I know. Me too. I wish I had a man here to hold me tight," I admitted.

"Call Tyson... oh yea, he blocked your number." Nessa giggled.

"That ain't funny!"

"I know because what if something came up? What if you needed his help with something or you had an emergency? That shit is real bogus when you think about it," she said.

"It really is. Then he done moved out of the hotel..."

BOOM!

All of a sudden, the lights went out. "Dammit!" I said as I got up to go look for a flashlight.

I was trying to feel along the walls and shit.

"What happened girl?" Nessa asked.

"My damn lights went out! Now I gotta find a freaking flashlight!"

"Uh, the one on your phone doesn't work?" she asked as she started laughing.

"Damn! I forgot!" I put the phone on speaker and turned on my flashlight. Then I went to the kitchen in search of candles and matches.

"Are you okay?" Nessa asked.

"Yea. I'm about to light some candles. Aren't your lights off too?"

"Nope. So far, so good."

"I should've gone to your place. Your lights never get cut off," I complained.

"That's not true. Sometimes, my lights go..."

"Sometimes your lights flicker on and off. Not the same thing."

"Girl, you need to log on to Facebook!"

"Why? What's going on?"

"Let's just say Trashelle finally responded," Nessa said.

"What?"

I hurried to light the candle and tried to rush to the sofa so I could log on to Facebook and find out what Nessa was talking about. I lit the candles and practically ran to the sofa.

POW!

"FUCK! OUCH!" I cried as I fell on the sofa and grabbed my right foot.

"What happened girl?"

"I stubbed my fucking toe on the coffee table!" I cried as tears threatened to fall.

"Are you okay?"

"No! That shit hurts!"

"Sorry cuz! You need to shake that shit off though and log on Facebook!" Nessa urged.

I put my painful feelings to the side and logged on to Facebook. I clicked my notifications and it showed me that Trashelle had commented on a post that I tagged her in. I quickly clicked on it.

Trashelle: The fact that you thought getting pregnant by Tyson was gonna bother me is hilarious! The only thing that did was give you more responsibilities. He doesn't even want you. He'll never be with your fat ass... that's the funniest part! You're already fat as fuck! Can you imagine how you're gonna look carrying a baby? What about after the baby comes? Tyson doesn't want you now, so he damn sure won't want you after you give birth... YOU SO STUPID!!

Trashelle finished it off with a bunch of laughing faces with the tears. That shit hurt me to the core because I knew I had a little extra meat on my bones, but Tyson said he liked that about me.

"You okay cuz?" Nessa asked, breaking into my thoughts.

"Yea. I just needed to catch my head for a second," I said as I brushed the tears away.

"You better not let that bitch get you down!"

"She ain't, but I'm sure that's what she was aiming for."

"Hell yea, it was!"

"I got something for that ass!" I said.

Thumbing through the gallery on my cell, I found a picture of Tyson lying in my bed asleep with a smile on his face. I had taken that picture of him when he was over here a few weeks ago. He didn't even know I had. I had just wanted it to remind myself that he and I had some good times and I hadn't imagined it all. Not that this baby inside me wasn't a constant reminder.

I uploaded the picture under her comment and posted a comment of my own.

Me: As you can see, Tyson was so content after being with me that he fell asleep with a smile on his face. I might be fat, but he wants me baby. If your skinny ass was all that, he would've never landed in my bed. Think about that the next time you come for me. I had "your" man and I'm carrying his son, so he's my man now bitch!

Trashelle waited a couple of minutes before she responded back.

Trashelle: He doesn't want you! Why can't you get that through your head and leave him alone?

Me: I'm not gonna continue going back and forth on social media with you about who Tyson wants. Once our kids are born, you will see who he wants. That shit will hit differently when he stops responding to your damn messages. Oh, he

probably already blocked your ass. Laugh now if you want to, but at the end of the day, I'll have the last laugh!!

Trashelle: Bitch go play in traffic or something!

Suddenly, the green light went off next to her name. I guess she logged off. I was sure she was feeling some kind of way after seeing that picture of Tyson in my bed. Maybe I took that part too far.

"You still there, cousin?" Nessa asked.

"Nessa I gotta go! I'll talk to you later."

With that I ended the call. I deleted the picture of Tyson but knew that bitch had probably took a screenshot already.

Yeah, I had probably fucked up with this stunt! Big Time!

Chapter Nine

Tyson

This weather was crazy as fuck. The thunder that was booming down on Houston was so strong that it shook the few pictures that hung on my bedroom wall.

Just as I got up to straighten them out, my phone started ringing. Since I had blocked both my baby mamas and anyone else that wasn't saved in my contacts, I picked it up and stared down at the screen because I still wasn't going to answer it until I saw that it was Johnson.

"Wassup man?"

"Aye, did you know yo baby mamas was cuttin' up on Facebook?" he asked.

"What are you talking about man?"

"I'm talking about Eraina and your girl, Trashelle, going at it about you on Facebook!"

"What?" I asked as I went to my laptop.

Hurrying to open it up, I logged onto Facebook.

"Where?"

"Go on Eraina's page. She posted a picture of her pregnancy test papers," Johnson informed me.

With my anger rising, I went to Eraina's page and sure enough there it was. A copy of her positive pregnancy test results was plastered all over Facebook for everyone to see. Then Eraina had the nerve to tag Trashelle in that shit. Trying to figure out exactly what was put out on the table, I went through the comments and saw that they were both acting the damn fools.

"Do you see the naked picture of you that Eraina posted? That's when I said I had to call you. That shit is messy as fuck!"

"The fuck! What naked picture?"

"In the comments under that post!"

"There's no naked picture of me under that post!" I said as I scratched my head thinking Johnson was losing his mind.

"What? She must have deleted it. Wait, I'm sending it to your phone because you know a nigga had to screenshot that shit!"

My phone dinged and a picture downloaded. Opening it up, my eyes widened. I couldn't believe that Eraina had took it there. To not only take a picture of me asleep in her bed, but to post it on social media. If that shit got around to my boss, I could lose my promotion and my job. Johnson was right, that shit was messy.

"Aye man, I'ma holla atchu!" I blurted out as I ended the call without giving him a chance to respond.

Dialing quickly, I called Eraina's number and waited for her to answer. "Hey baby," she sang like things were all good after she posted all that crap on social media.

"Eraina what the fuck is going on with you?"

"What do you mean babe?"

"I'm talking about that shit you been posting on Facebook!"

"What? I just posted to let everybody know that I was pregnant..."

"Okay, if that's true, why the fuck did you tag Trashelle in your bullshit?!"

"Bullshit? So, me being pregnant is bullshit?" she asked. "I-I-I"

"You know how messy that shit looks? Then you posted a pic of me sleeping in your fuckin' bed! Why would you do that shit?" I asked. "What the fuck were you thinking?"

"Tyson..."

"No, don't fuckin' Tyson me! What the hell are you doing Eraina? You wanna know what the fuck you doing? You making me regret that I was ever with you! You're even making me think twice about having a baby with you!" I said and I wasn't lying either.

The shit she was doing was reckless and childish. We were grown ass people, and her and

Tray were acting like fucking teenagers. I couldn't believe she had actually taken it that far.

"I'm sorry. I wasn't thinking..."

"Shit, I know that! This is the reason I blocked y'all asses in the first place. Y'all too fuckin' childish! Y'all make a nigga not wanna be nowhere around y'all!" I continued.

"Look Tyson!" Eraina stated sternly until I quieted down enough for her to speak. "I was wrong for posting all that shit, but I don't know what came over me, honestly. Since I got pregnant, I've been more emotional than I have in my life and all I can say is I'm truly sorry. I didn't do it to hurt you Tyson. I did it because I was hurt..."

"Hurt how Eraina?"

"Hurt because you chose to tell me everything but hide me from Trashelle like I was the plague or some shit," she countered. "It's like you're proud that she's pregnant but embarrassed about me carrying your baby. I don't get it... I mean, I understand that you and her were together for years, but I've known you for a very long time too. Maybe not on that level, but once we reached it, I thought we had a serious connection. At least I did on my part."

"It's nothing like that Eraina. I'm not embarrassed about you having my seed. I'm embarrassed about being careless enough to have two women pregnant at the same time. What does that say about me?" I blurted out before I could catch myself. The verbal admission created a lump in the bottom of my stomach and regret followed.

"I'm surprised to hear you say that, but you shouldn't be embarrassed Tyson. The way you handle it from here on out will shift everyone's opinion... not that they matter."

"You are so fucking right Eraina, but all this nonsense has to stop. Especially before these babies come."

"Well, stop blocking my calls, check on me frequently and spend some quality time with me on occasion and I promise not to act a fool," Eraina teased.

Shit, I didn't know what she meant by that last part because I had no intention on being back with her in an intimate situation. What happened, happened, but I wasn't trying to be with her or Tray like that. Both of them weren't even a relationship option. Hell, honestly, I was still trying to get at Miss Tanya Shaw no matter how hopeless it seemed at the moment.

"Did you hear me Tyson?"

"Yeah, but that ain't good enough..."

"What?!"

"It ain't good enough Eraina! I want you to delete all your social media pages until after you have the baby!"

"What about all the milestones of my pregnancy?! I want all my friends and family to stay updated!" Eraina whined.

"Save all your pictures and post them afterwards! As far as your friends and family are concerned, text them!" I demanded. "Both of our jobs are on the line for even fucking around like that Eraina! Who's gonna take care of our baby if we both get fired?"

"I can just apply for a job on another platform Tyson!"

Damn, that was the best suggestion that Eraina had come up with since I got her ass pregnant. Happy as hell that she came up with that plan, I hurried up and agreed with her.

"You know TransOil is hiring and that rig is near ours. You can still stay in Houston and be near enough for me to see my kid often."

"So, you don't think that we'll ever be together Tyson?" Eraina asked.

"We'll always be a part of each other's life because of our baby. For that, I'll always have love for you and respect you. Just as long as you don't keep doing that dumb shit..."

"I said that I wouldn't, and I'll delete all my social media pages, but you have to stick to your side of the deal too Tyson. As soon as this two-week hitch is over and I transfer to a different company, I want you to make it clear to Trashelle that I'm just as entitled as she is and our baby is just as important as your kid with her. Can you do that Tyson? Can you make sure she knows that?" Eraina pressed then smacked her lips.

"I gotcha and I'll come check on you tomorrow. Is that cool?"

"Yes, I'll be home."

Ending the call, I was feeling a little good about myself and how I was handling things. Just not good enough to unblock Tray and hear her mouth. Not only would she have a million questions for me, she would talk shit about me calling her a ho' when I was out there fucking another woman. It wasn't that I went bareback though. It was totally a technicality. Something had to go wrong with the one of the condoms that Eraina and I had used.

Either way, I didn't choose to contact Tray until the day before I was leaving for my hitch. That way I didn't have to deal with her mouth or bad attitude for more than I had to.

"You're just now calling me? Why haven't you come by Tyson? You don't even give a damn about me or our baby!" Tray screamed.

"This is the reason!" I snapped. "Every time I call or come by this is the shit I have to deal with Tray! I don't wanna hear all that bickering!"

"Well, you're gonna hear it after what that bitch Eraina told me!" she cried. "How could you Tyson?"

"See, here we go..."

"No! Here you go! You calling me a fucking ho' when you're out there sticking your dick in other women raw!"

"You don't even know what the hell you're talking about Tray!"

"I know you got two women pregnant at the same time with the exact same due date! That means you were fucking us both on the same day!"

"Now you sound stupid! Just because you guys have the same due date doesn't mean..."

"It means that you were fucking us both raw around the same time and that's just as bad Tyson! No matter how you try to spin it!"

"Tray, I was just calling to check on you..."

"You need to be doing more than that! More than a week done went by and this is all I'm getting? A fucking phone call? And you probably been laying up with Eraina's big dinosaur ass! Taking care of that bitch and why?!"

"Now yo' ass is really going to the left!"

"No Tyson! You are!" Tray hollered. "You moved and I don't even know where you live! You blocked my number so I can't call you from any phone! You haven't come by to check on me..."

"This is why Tray! I can't take all the yelling and disrespectful shit! You ain't got to be cussing me out and shit, but you are! I fucked up and now I'm having two kids! I'm the one who has to deal with it while you and Eraina wanna keep whining and shit..."

"*So, you have been with her!*" Tray cried.

"That's it! I'll call you tomorrow before I leave to check on you, but right now, I can't listen to all this..."

"Fuck you Tyson!"

Without giving her a response, I simply hung up and kept her ass on block. Evidently, she wasn't ready to play nice.

Without a worry in the world, I took my ass to sleep and slept all through the night. I didn't get up until my alarm went off and I hit 'snooze' three times. Then I had to end up rushing to the docks.

"Shit!" I grunted as soon as I parked and got out of my car.

Eraina's friend Nessa was dropping her off. When she saw me, she just had to get out. All I kept thinking was that they better not be up to no wild shit especially after Eraina vowed to keep things calm and on the low.

"Hey," they both sang out as I walked by.

"Can you help me with this bag, please Tyson," Eraina asked nicely.

Picking it up with a smile and a nod, I gripped the duffle and turned to speak to Nessa but before I could get a word out, there came Tray. She came straight up to us with a scowl.

Eraina was cool about it when she approached. It was her homegirl Nessa that wasn't feeling Tray's negative vibe. Once they began exchanging words, there wasn't anything I could do but try to get in between them.

Why the hell did I do that?

Chapter Ten

Nessa

That bitch Trashelle really tried me at the docks. I already didn't like the ho' behind the little comments she left on Eraina's post. She was bougie and thought her shit didn't stink. I was just the person to put her in her place by bragging on how my homegirl was about to have Tyson's baby.

"Bitch I don't know why you looking at me like I did you something! I don't even know yo ugly ass!" she yelled at me because I was eyeballing her.

"Ugly?! Bitch have you looked in the mirror lately?" I asked as me and Eraina started laughing. "You have that ol' pit bull mug that only a mother could love! I'on know what Tyson saw in yo ugly tail! Especially that tired ass blonde wig you wearin'!"

"Bitch fuck you! You need to worry about those charges against yo ass!"

What the fuck? Who told that bitch I had charges on me?

"I can read the paper bitch! You'd wanna watch ya step before I plaster yo mugshot all over social media!" Trashelle threatened. "This don't even concern you. It's between me and that buffalo you call a friend!"

"Buffalo?" Eraina asked. "Bitch fuck you! Standing there looking like a damn cooked noodle!"

I guess that pissed Trashelle off because do you know that bitch tried to swing on me? Yeah, I tried to tear her head off too! She was lucky that Tyson got between us and held me back! I swear I wanted to beat the breaks off her with her reckless ass mouth!

"What the fuck is wrong with y'all yo? Y'all trying to get me fired?" Tyson asked as he looked from me to Trashelle to Eraina.

"You better get yo bitch because I ain't the one for her to be playing with!" I told him.

"Do you not see that she's pregnant?" he asked with a furious look on his face.

"Do I look like I give a fuck if that ho' pregnant? She ain't carrying my baby!" I yelled.

"You got one mo' time to call me out my name BITCH!!" Trashelle said.

I was about to haul off on her ass, but the only thing that saved her was security. They were already familiar with her too. The tall one called her out about pushing Eraina in the water the last time. They couldn't wait to escort her off the premises and trespass her ass again.

Not wanting anything else to do with the escalating situation once I saw those handcuffs come out, I got to stepping. I wasn't a fool and I wasn't about to get locked up behind beating a pregnant ho'!

Taking myself right on home, I laughed to myself about how Trashelle made a fool of herself. The shit was funny on so many levels.

Being so wrapped up in what had just happened, I didn't pay attention when I got to my apartment and pulled up to the mailboxes. There was a familiar car, but I didn't notice it until Byron was climbing out. The frown on his face warned me that his visit wasn't friendly.

Fiddling with my keyring, I quickly got a grip on my pepper spray and flipped the safety latch off. Positioning my finger on the button, I got ready to spray.

"Nessa, I'm not about to play with you!" Byron whispered as he got closer to me.

"Who's playing! I'm tired of all this shit with you and your wife. Go ahead and be with her! I'm done!"

"Then destroy all that shit you have on me!" Byron demanded with a strong stench of alcohol on his breath.

"Go home, you're drunk!"

"Destroy the shit Nessa! I don't need it hanging over my head!"

"You should've thought about all that before you played with my heart! You promised to be with me!"

There I went pouring out my heart like a damn dummy, knowing Byron was no good for me. He was no good for anyone! Cold hearted bastard wanted me to kill his unborn kid! I had to remind myself of that so I could toughen up and cuss his ass out for even coming at me like that.

"Fuck off Byron and leave me alone!" I hissed, ready to just walk away. Only I couldn't. That fool wanted to put his hands on me and spin me around like he was crazy!

That was just why he got sprayed down to the ground. The only bad thing about it all was that I got misted a little too. It was enough to send me running to my apartment. Hell, I even left my car parked in the visitor's spot in front of the rental office.

Locking myself inside, I ran to the bathroom and rinsed my face for the next 10 minutes. My eyes were on fire and my skin was irritated to the point that I was ready to go to the emergency room.

If you thought all that was bad, 10 minutes after that, that bitch Regina was at my door. I couldn't believe that little maggot had the nerve to call his wife like she was going to do something! Popping up at my place uninvited, she was going to mess around and get served with a fucking 2-piece fucking with a ghetto bitch like me!

"OPEN THE DOOR BITCH!!" she yelled from the outside.

Shit, hell yeah, I opened the door. If she thought I was scared of her and about to hide behind a door, she had me fucked up. I pulled that door back ready to fuck her up.

"BITCH FUCK YOU!!"

"That's why I called the cops on your dumb ass!"

"YOU CALLED THE COPS ON ME BITCH?! HOW THE FUCK YOU CALL THE COPS ON ME?!!" I was livid. Like that nigga approached me talking stupid and putting his hands on me. He had me fucked up!

"BITCH YOU SPRAYED MY HUSBAND WITH PEPPER SPRAY!! THE COPS COMING FOR YOUR ASS!"

"Fuck you and that raggedy piece of shit! He put his hands on me, so he got sprayed and if you don't get the hell off my doorstep, you'll be next!" I threatened while rubbing my eyes.

They were still stinging like crazy because I had that police pepper spray. That shit had the potential to blind my ass. I was glad it only misted me and not gotten too much in my eyes. I guess that was why I didn't see when Regina stole on me. Busted me right in the left eye!

"Bitch!" I hollered trying to see where to swing. It was too late. She got in three good punches and darted. I couldn't have caught her if I tried. Shit, I couldn't even see straight!

Oh, how I was going to get her and Byron for this shit! Regina was about to find out all about how her husband, the one who she was fighting for, was trying to kill her baby!

"IF ONLY YOU KNEW BITCH!! IF ONLY YOU KNEW WHAT THAT NIGGA WAS CAPABLE OF!!" I shouted as she stood near her car joining her stupid ass husband as he showered himself with gallons of water.

That shit looked like some ghetto ass bullshit. I was tempted to tell her the truth right then and there, but I decided to keep shit under wraps just a little while longer.

The nerve of Byron bringing his drunk ass over here.

To think, this fool actually thought I was going to get rid of my evidence. He was sadly mistaken if he thought that was going to work.

Oh, and his wife Regina, she was in for a rude awakening if she thought a baby was going to keep their marriage together. That marriage wouldn't survive shit because Byron didn't want the same things she did. He didn't want a baby with her. He didn't want to even be with her.

If Byron was living in that house with his wife again, I bet the only reason was so he could make sure the job got done. I wasn't a fool. I knew that nigga was up to something with his shady ass.

"I got something for both them bitches!" I huffed as I turned and went inside my apartment.

I didn't have time for their shenanigans. What was going on with those stupid ass niggas anyway? First, I had to deal with Trashelle and Tyson's dumb asses and that shit had nothing to do with me. That was Eraina's battle, but because she was my best friend and pregnant, I felt the need to try and protect her. Next time, she was on her own though. I couldn't get wrapped up in her shit no more.

With every step I made, I needed to be careful to stay out of trouble. Thanks to Byron, I had a legal case of my own to deal with, so I couldn't afford a second charge when I was still battling the first one.

Truthfully, ever since that bitch Regina said she had called the cops, I was waiting for them to come knock on my damn door at any given moment. It was the last thing I needed but that shit was self- defense, so I shouldn't have even been worried about it one bit.

As I sat there thinking, I start seeing things from a different angle. Like, if the cops did come knocking on my door to try and jam me up about me spraying Byron, what if I showed them all of those messages between us.

Yeah, let them come knock on my damn door. I'ma show 'em.

Chapter Eleven

Byron

That bitch had a lot of nerve spraying me with that fucking pepper spray. The only thing I wanted to do was talk to her about clearing all that evidence out of her phone. She was pissed off at me, so the last thing I needed was for her to take that shit to the police and get my ass locked the fuck up. A woman scorned could be a really bad thing. But if Nessa was to be stupid and show those receipts, I would make sure I killed her ass before I got locked up.

Yeah, I probably made it worse when I called my wife Regina to come and get me, but hell, I didn't have any other choice. I couldn't see to drive myself home. I couldn't even see where I was to find water to flush my eyes out. If it hadn't been for OnStar, I wouldn't have been able to contact Regina at all. Using a bottled water that was in my car from I don't know when, I began washing my eyes until my wife showed up minutes later. By then, it felt like I was approaching blindness.

Thinking smartly, Regina showed up with several gallons of water and began pouring the water over my face. I was in so much pain, I didn't know if I'd ever be able to see again. Why would Nessa do some shit like that when all I was trying to do was talk to her? She said she loved me, but when she did that shit there was no love shown.

As I stood there with mixed emotions and in severe pain, all Regina wanted to do was keep arguing about calling the police. I couldn't let her do that because I was on private property. If my wife contacted the police, I'd most likely end up in jail.

"I'm gonna call the police!" Regina fumed for the fifth time.

"For what?" I asked as I tried to get my eyes to focus.

"Because that bitch sprayed you with mace! Are you fucking kidding me right now?"

"No, but that shit ain't necessary!"

"What do you mean?"

"I mean, look where the hell we are Regina! I ain't even supposed to be over here!"

"Right! So, why are you here Byron?"

"Because I needed to talk to Nessa about some business we had started before shit went left!"

"Business? What business could you possibly have with that bitch?"

"We had some business to discuss and that's all you need to know!" I said.

"You're still fucking her! After everything that bitch has done to you, you're still fucking her!!" Regina hissed like she could spit fire.

"Are you outta yo damn mind!" I fussed. "I don't have time for this shit!"

Walking over to my second car, I opened the door to get in. Regina immediately started yelling again with that annoying ass voice of hers.

"Where the hell do you think you're going?"

"Away from you!"

"This is how you do me Byron? When I'm pregnant with your baby!!" she cried.

"I didn't ask for that baby! Don't be acting like I wanted you to get pregnant! We don't fuck! We don't make love! We don't even live together, so I don't know how you expected a baby to fix our marriage!! Hell, right now, I don't even like you very much!" I confessed with no hesitation because by then, I was fed up with everything.

Standing there in tears, Regina began balling her eyes out like her heart was breaking. I guess it was false when they said words didn't hurt because mine definitely seemed to be hurting Regina to the core, but I couldn't help the way I felt. Besides, I was tired of playing the role.

"You probably hate to hear this shit Regina, but I never wanted kids with you! I wish you would've aborted that baby when you could have because the last thing I want is to be tied to you for 18 plus years! Hell, I don't wanna be tied to you another minute to be truthful! We should've been done got a damn divorce!"

Tears rained down her face as I slid in the driver's seat of my car. Regina could kiss the crack of my ass if she thought I was going to feel sad about that shit.

"I don't know why I ever thought this marriage with you would work out! You're too much of a selfish bastard for that to happen!"

"Bastard? I'm not a bastard, but that baby you're carrying will be!" I threatened as I started my ride.

"MAKE SURE YOU GOT SOMEWHERE ELSE TO STAY BECAUSE I DON'T WANT YOU COMING BACK TO MY FUCKING HOUSE!!"

"For one thing, I don't live there! I got a place to lay my head!" I spoke calmly. "But don't get it twisted about OUR house while you up here talking about it's yours!"

"You got me fucked up Byron and you heard what I said! MY HOUSE!!"

"Bitch I still pay the bills in that muthafucka in case I need to remind you!!" I fussed.

"BITCH?! OH, SO NOW THE MOTHER OF YOUR CHILD IS A BITCH?!" she hollered.

"That's what you acting like!"

Next thing I knew, she had ran up on me and punched my ass smack dab in the face. Gotdammit! I hadn't even seen that shit coming.

"You lucky I don't wanna go to jail!" I snapped with a scowl then put my car in reverse and backed out the parking spot. I hit the gas and sped out of the parking lot on two fucking wheels.

It was unbelievable how bad shit had gotten. First, that bitch Nessa had sprayed me in the face with some mace. As if that shit wasn't bad enough, I called my wife for help and that bitch done run up on me. Like, I couldn't win for shit!

Clearing my head, I hit up Nessa because I still needed her to get rid of all that shit in her phone. She didn't answer the first, second, or third times I called. However, I wasn't about to give up. She had too much incriminating evidence on me for me to just say fuck it.

Trying to dial Nessa up again, I listened to it ring 3 times. Finally, I got lucky and she picked up.

"Why the hell do you keep calling me?! I told you I'm done with you and your bullshit Byron!"

"That's fine! You can be done with me. All I want is for you to delete those messages from your phone," I said sweetly.

"What messages are you referring to?" she asked in a tone just as sweet.

That's that bullshit I'm talking about!

"You know exactly what messages I'm talking about Nessa! C'mon man, why you playing games with me and shit?"

"Oh, I'm not the one playing games. That would be your ass! I don't know what messages you're talking about," she claimed.

"I'm talking about OUR messages! The thread of messages between me and you or you and I, however that shit goes! I just want those messages gone!" I explained.

"Oh, you mean the messages where you gave me instructions on how to get your wife to miscarry your baby? Those messages?" she asked with a chuckle.

"C'mon ma, why you gotta be like that? At one point you said you loved me and would do anything for me..."

"HA!! That ship has sailed boy! I can't stand your grimy ass now!"

"Wow! Really Nessa?"

"Yeah, really! You sent my ass to jail Byron!"

"You fucked up my car! You know how many hours I spent fixing that car up? It was like you just said fuck me when you took that bat to it!"

"That's exactly what I said then and that's what I'm saying now. Ever since we got together Byron, you've caused nothing but drama and chaos in my life. I don't want that shit no more. You can stay with your wife, kill the baby, whatever you wanna do, but leave me out of it. I want nothing more to do with you..."

"If that's true, just delete the messages and you won't ever hear from me again!"

"No, I need those messages for insurance..."

"Insurance? What fucking insurance?" I asked as I scratched my head. She was confusing the fuck out of me right now.

"Insurance that you will stay away from me and out of my life. Oh yea, and you better go drop those charges..."

"I told you that I did that already!"

"And you betta not be fucking lying Byron!"

"Delete the messages ma, please. I'm asking you, but I won't keep asking you for much longer..."

"Is that a threat Byron? Are you threatening me?"

"Take it how you like, but I'm tired of this sick twisted game you keep playing with me. Delete the fucking messages and send me a screenshot, and I won't bother you again. Keep the messages and I will continue to pursue you until..."

"Until what?"

"You don't really want the answer to that question ma. Just delete the messages," I warned before I ended the call.

Nessa was really trying my fucking patience right now, but she needed to know that I wasn't playing games. She had evidence that could get me locked the fuck up for the rest of my life because I still had plans to kill that baby and possibly my wife too. I mean, why not? She was on some bullshit anyway. How the fuck she gone tell me to stay away from our house when I was still paying bills there? That wasn't even possible because it didn't make sense.

But after everything that happened, I decided to give her some space. Shit, I needed some for myself so I could think things through. I needed to figure out my next move and where to go from here.

Now that it wasn't cool to go back to the house that I once shared with Regina, I headed to the house I was staying at temporarily. That shit was playing out too, so before my living situation flopped completely, I packed all my shit and rented a room at the Holiday Inn. I needed to shower, change and lay low for the next couple of weeks or so. There were some things I needed to figure out.

I certainly couldn't do it with those two nagging bitches in my ear.

Chapter Twelve

Trashelle

Eraina's homegirl, that 'Nessa' bitch, had the nerve to put her hands on me?! Then to get escorted and trespassed off the property indefinitely humiliated me to the core. Had me so damn mad that my hands were shaking, and I was thinking of doing some crazy shit to Eraina.

"She don't deserve to have Tyson's baby! Had she kept the shit between her legs a secret then none of this would ever have happened. But no! Eraina had to share her shit with a man that already had a woman! A man that was already trying to get me pregnant! Me! Not her!" I cried once I got in the car and pounded on the steering wheel.

The pain of knowing that some other chick was having a baby by Tyson was killing me inside. No matter how much I cried about it, no one truly understood what I was going through. Nobody seemed to be on my side.

"Maybe I should just have a fucking abortion! Maybe I should just kill my fucking self too!" I shouted with my feelings flowing out of control.

Okay, maybe I was going overboard with saying that I was going to kill myself, but after finding out that Eraina was having a baby by Tyson too... I didn't know if I could deal with that for the rest of my life. Another baby by another woman?! Fighting for the attention of a man that betrayed both of us?!

Tyson was at fault in all this but steadily wanted to play the victim. That fucker didn't even come to my rescue when security took me away kicking and screaming. I was the damn victim!

"I can't!" I screamed out as I finally drove off the lot and went in the direction of my house.

Honestly, I didn't even want to go there and be reminded of Tyson. Every single time I walked in the front door of my place, I could still smell the scent of his cologne lingering in the air.

Damn him!

It wasn't fair that I would have to be the one to give up my child by aborting it, then Eraina would win and I would be left with nothing. It was her who needed to bow down and schedule her visit to the nearest Planned Parenthood Clinic or whoever did those fetal terminations because I wasn't going!

"What am I gonna do?" I cried as I drew my car up into the driveway. "Maybe I should just beat her ass!"

Two weeks! Two weeks I would have to wait to see both of them! Two weeks that Eraina had to spend with Tyson! How was I going to survive 14 damn days without knowing what was going on between them?

Still in tears, I forced myself into the house and literally threw my tired body onto my bed. There was nothing I could do to stop the crying. I was beside myself with so much grief, you could've sworn someone had died. Then I found myself hyperventilating.

To calm myself down, I stripped down and hopped in the shower. As I stepped in and allowed the hot streams of water to penetrate my skin, I started to relax. To my surprise, the salty drops of warm liquid finally stopped flowing.

"I'm stronger than this! I can do this! My mama raised me by myself... but then again, my daddy didn't have any other kids either.

However, I looked at my situation, the only thing that would make me feel better was if Eraina got an abortion. I was even considering bribing the bitch with every dime I had. Then Tyson would have no choice but to take care of me and my baby.

"I'm so confused right now!" I huffed as I stepped out of the shower. I searched through my bedroom dresser drawer and found a pair of pajamas to put on.

It was early in the morning and I was getting right back in my bed. That was where I planned on staying for the next two weeks until Tyson came back. That was just enough time to figure out how I was going to deal with my problem... Eraina.

*****

Two Weeks Later...

Making it to the docks in the rental I got the night before, I parked on the dark side of the lot wearing a black wig and sunglasses. Instead of waiting for Tyson to appear, I was more concerned with Eraina. Figuring that her homegirl Nessa would be picking her up, I sat off in the cut until I saw her pull up and park near the ramp. Right next to Tyson's truck.

"I should just go over there and catch her off guard with a blow to her skull!" I whispered to myself as I listened closely to my car quietly idling. I had to be prepared to pull off at any given second.

If Tyson strolled his ass down that ramp with Eraina, I didn't think I could stick to the plan. The more anxious I became, the more I wanted to hop out the car and be ready to jump her ass.

The only reason I didn't make a move right then was the sight of the security guys roaming the lot. I hurried up and changed my mind because if they spotted me, I would surely go to jail. Not to mention, get more embarrassed than I did the last time and I definitely didn't need that.

Glancing upward as I heard loud voices, I saw Tyson walking down the ramp with his boy Johnson. They were joking and laughing, but I wasn't once I spotted Nessa pulling up to get Eraina's punk ass.

As my eyes gazed upon Tyson's side chick strutting off the ramp next, my skin began to itch. "This muthafucka betta not even look her way!"

Watching closely back and forth, I saw Tyson get in his truck and pull off before Eraina could even make it to the cement path that went to the parking lot. Revving my engine, I put the gear in 'drive' and raced forward. I wanted so badly to run that bitch over before she got to her friend Nessa's car, but something suddenly stopped me before I made impact.

I was not sure if it was the gut feeling that hit me, or the sight of those same two security cars that were coming my way. Whichever it was, I swerved my car as soon as I got inches away from hitting her and peeled out of the lot before the rent-a-cops could even think about catching me.

Buzzzzz...

My cell suddenly rang, and the screen lit up the whole car! I quickly answered when I saw that it was Tyson calling.

"Hey Tray, I just wanted to reach out and let you know that I've had nothing but time to think over the past two weeks. I unblocked your number and I'm not gonna do that shit no more. All I want is for us to get along..."

"So, you're coming home?" I asked as I anxiously scrunched down in my seat.

"Tray, I got my own house now, you know that. Besides, I think it's best if we just work on being friends for now. I don't think that we should be in a relationship anymore because clearly that ain't been working for us. We need to be in a better place with each other before our baby comes..."

"And what about Eraina and your baby with her...?"

"Let's keep that separate from what we got going on. One has nothing to do with the other. I already had a long talk with Eraina and told her that even though y'all don't like each other, y'all need to respect one another..."

"You want me to respect that bitch?"

"Why she gotta be a bitch though Tray?" he asked. "This shit that's going on between all of us right now is my doing, not yours or hers. Y'all need to stop punishing and disrespecting each other because of something that I did! I'm responsible for all this shit, but y'all blaming each other and that shit ain't cool!"

"Whatever!"

"I bet if you guys had a conversation, y'all would see that y'all have a lot in common. Shit, y'all would probably even like each other..."

"NEVER!! I'll never like that bitch!"

"You're not ever gonna try huh?"

"I don't need to try. As long as she keeps her distance from me, we'll be good. So, how are we gonna build our friendship if you don't come home Tyson?" I whined ready to break down in tears.

"Tray, please don't start that again. I really want this to work, but the only way that can happen is if you try things my way. Let me take care of you the best I can without you trying to dictate my every move. I can't have you worrying about where I am, where I was, or who I'm with because that hasn't been your business for quite a while..."

"You're my man and about to be the father of my baby..."

"See, here you go Tray. We're not together..."

"So, I can see other people like you do, right Tyson? It's okay for me to go out and fuck another nigga and let him nut up on your unborn baby's head huh?! Is that what you're saying?" I spat pushing Tyson to the limit.

"This is what I'm talking about Tray!"

"So, can I? Can I fuck another nigga while I'm carrying your baby Tyson?!"

"No, that shit is foul!"

"Well, what the hell do you call what you're doing? You're fucking me and Eraina..."

"I'll tell you what Tray, you don't have sex with nobody else until after you have the baby and I won't either."

"But we'll be having sex the whole time though, right? You won't be fucking Eraina too, will you?"

"No, I'm not gonna have sex with either one of you..."

"So, you think I'm just supposed to go without?!" I shrieked with the thought of not getting dick for the next six damn months! Was this nigga crazy?!

"Oh, I guess with your track record of fucking, that's gonna be hard for you..."

"You muthafucka you!" I hissed ready to go off, but I had that insult coming so I stopped right there.

"Tray, I didn't call to argue with you. In fact, I was gonna come and take you to breakfast so we can talk."

"Not if you're gonna keep hitting me with them lame ass ho' blows!" I huffed.

"Nah, that was uncalled for and I apologize for that, Tray. Just come to breakfast so we can work out some kind of plan for these next few months..."

"Yeah, okay," I agreed before we made plans then hung up.

Was Tyson that stupid? Did he really think that he could split his time equally with both me and Eraina? Did he plan on going to all her doctor's appointments and mine too? Or was he dumb enough to think that we would make ours on the same day at the same place so he could kill two birds with one stone?

Either way I looked at things, I couldn't see myself sharing Tyson with Eraina or any other bitch. He was going to have to make a decision even if it meant I had to give him an ultimatum. It was going to be me or her and today, he would have to choose.

Breaking out in laughter as I did 70mph on the main road, I thought about how Eraina's eyes bucked when she saw it was me in the black car. I didn't give a damn either because I was sure they didn't get to see my plates with all the dust and dirt the rental car kicked up.

All I knew was, I was glad that she saw it was me. That should let her know that I could've killed her ass if I wanted to. That should let her know that I wasn't the bitch to be played with. She had better be glad that Jesus took the wheel on that one because had he not taken it, I would've laid her fat ass out!

"Let me take this car back to the rental place!" I giggled as I raced to Enterprise Rental to return the Ford and hop in my Chevy.

It was time to go meet Tyson and see what the hell he was talking about. If it wasn't anything that I wanted to hear, he could kiss the thought of having a baby with me goodbye. One thing I wasn't about to do was share a baby daddy or act like a sister wife. He had me fucked up if he thought that was about to go down.

That's one thing I'm sure of!

Chapter Thirteen

Eraina

The last couple of weeks on the rig with Tyson was just what I needed, or so I thought. I was prepared to give him some good-good during our stint on the rig but as it turned out, he didn't want it. Instead, he wanted to talk about our future raising our child together. That conversation didn't go anything like how I hoped.

"You wanna talk about us?" I asked.

"Yea..."

"So, you're choosing me?" I asked, getting excited.

"I'm choosing our child."

"What?"

"I want us to talk about how we're going to co-parent our child Eraina," he said.

"And I wanna talk about us getting back together to do that," I said.

"We aren't getting back together because we were never a couple..."

"What? Sure, we were a couple. I mean, when you broke up with Trashelle's ass, who was there for you, huh? Who was there to comfort, coddle and fuck you every day huh?" I asked.

"That doesn't make us a couple. We were two friends having sex and enjoying each other's company..."

"Oh, is that what you call it?"

"Yes. Look Eraina, I'm not trying to hurt you. I just don't want you reading too much into shit with us. We weren't a couple and we aren't going to be one. I just want to be there for you to help you raise the baby," he said.

"Wow! This is some bullshit Tyson and you know it!" I cried.

My heart was breaking into so many pieces, I just knew he could hear them. Why was he doing this to me? Why was he treating me like some second- rate random bitch off the streets? I knew that I had meant something to him, so why was he acting like I didn't?

"Please don't make this out to be more than it really was. I wanna be there for you as you go through your pregnancy. I'll go to the doctor's appointments with you and everything. I'm going to be there for you..."

"And her too!!" I cried, referring to Trashelle. "Are you getting back together with her Tyson?"

"I'm not getting back together with anyone. I only want to be there for my children... point blank, period!"

"Uh huh. We'll see," I said as I bolted from his room.

That happened the third day we arrived on the rig, and I had been keeping my distance ever since.

To be honest, I was a little disappointed and a lot hurt that Tyson didn't want to be with me. Hell, what was wrong with him?! I was carrying his first son, his only son! I mean, I didn't know it for sure, but I was almost positive when it would be time for an ultrasound, they would tell us that we were having a baby boy. Why didn't he want to be with me?

I had done my best not to think about that bitch Trashelle the whole time we were on the rig. I practiced that saying, "Out of sight, out of mind". Too bad she hadn't practiced the same thing. As I was walking towards Nessa's car, a black Ford almost ran me the fuck over. When I saw that it was Trashelle driving that car, I was tempted to call the cops and have her ass arrested.

I couldn't believe that bitch was at the docks waiting for me. And the fact that she tried to hit me with a fucking car really said a lot about her sanity. She had to be crazy to do some shit like that.

"Who the hell was that?!" Nessa yelled as she jumped out of the car and rushed over to me Before she could get me in the car, one of the security guards pulled up.

He rolled his window down and asked, "Are you alright?" It was James, an attractive but older gentleman. I mean, he wasn't that old. Probably in his mid- 30's I suppose.

"Yea, I'm okay," I said as I blew out an exasperated breath.

He hopped out of the car with a bottle of water. "Here you go," he offered.

"Thanks," I said as I took the bottle from his hand and took a sip.

"Did you see who was driving that car?"

I shook my head 'no' as I continued to sip on the cool water. "I wasn't able to get a good look," I lied.

"Wow! Whoever it was almost ran you over," he commented as he stared at me with concern written all over his face. "People drive like they're crazy out here!"

"I know. Thank God they didn't bump me."

"I'm gonna call the police and give them a description of the car. Maybe they can find the person who was driving," James said.

"That's okay. You don't have to go through all that trouble," I said.

"What? Are you sure?" James asked.

"Yea, I'm sure. I'm fine, and after a long two-week stint, I just wanna go home and relax," I said.

"Okay, but if you change your mind, just hit me up," James offered.

"Thanks again James. See you in two," I acknowledged as he waved goodbye and got in his car.

"James is sweet on you," Nessa teased.

"Girl bye! He was just doing his job!"

"Bullshit! He likes you!"

"Forget all that," I hissed as we got inside her car. "I saw the bitch that was driving that car!"

"What? But you said…"

"Forget what I told James. It was that bitch Trashelle who tried to run me over!" I huffed trying to pull myself together because I nearly pissed in my coveralls!

Nessa stabbed it off soon as I strapped myself in the seatbelt. "No way!" she screamed.

"Yes way!"

"Oh, I got something for that bitch!!"

She was trying to catch up to Trashelle, but I knew that was impossible. "No!"

"What the hell do you mean no?! That bitch almost killed you and the baby Eraina!"

"I know. Just let her go!" I insisted. "First of all, you're not going to catch her. She's long gone by now sis. Second, I got another way to get at her."

"What?"

"Well, at the rate she's going, Trashelle is gonna hang herself. She's gonna either lose that baby or land her ass in jail fucking with me. One thing I know for sure is she ain't gonna end up with Tyson! No matter how you look at it, she's gonna lose!"

"Why are you so sure of that Eraina?"

"Because Tyson and I had a long talk..."

"So, y'all together? That nigga promised to be with you?" Nessa probed as she slowed down and obeyed the speed limit.

"No, but..."

"But what?"

"Well, we not only came to an understanding that he would take care of me, but he promised that he would always be there for me and my baby," I began to explain. "No, it's not a promise to be with me, but it's a start. Nessa, you may think that I'm dumb for sharing Tyson, but I don't see it that way. I see it as an opportunity to show him how understanding and patient I can be. I want him to see another side of me... a softer side."

"So, what's your plan Eraina?"

"First, I'm going to get my hair done and buy me a cute dress for tonight!" I giggled, forgetting all about how Trashelle just tried to run me over.

"What's going on tonight?"

"He's taking me to dinner!" I bragged. "He's never really seen me all dolled up, so I'm hoping to catch his eye tonight, then his heart later on..."

"No, yo ass is tryna catch that dick! Bitch who you think you foolin'?" Nessa clowned, turning up the music as we hit the block leading to my apartment.

After she dropped me off, I sat for a minute to rethink the plan I had previously come up with. I had no idea if Tyson was going to even come back to the apartment with me or not. All I knew was that I was horny and in love with my baby daddy. Now I knew how Nessa felt when Byron approached her to make his wife miscarry. Of course, I wasn't thinking about anything along those lines where Trashelle was concerned. But it would make things a lot easier for me and Tyson to be together if her and her baby were out of the picture.

However, the last thing I wanted to do was make Trashelle lose Tyson's baby. I didn't like the fact that she was carrying his baby, but what could I do about that? Sure, I wanted her to lose the baby, but I wasn't about to do anything drastic to get me locked up in prison.

I just knew that with the right amount of persuasion, Tyson would forget all about Trashelle and be all mine. Why wouldn't he want to be with me anyway? I was the better woman for him. She was a ho' while I held a decent job. She was carrying what I hoped was a girl while I was giving

Tyson a son. I just had to be! I mean, what man wouldn't want a son?

I didn't know what the future held for me and Tyson, but what I did know was that I loved him, and I wanted this relationship to work. We had to get back on the right track for our baby's sake.

We just had to...

Chapter Fourteen

Trashelle

I had to admit that talking to Tyson gave me a different perspective on my future. He wanted to be with me but didn't want to sleep with me. He wanted me to be his baby mama but didn't want me to sleep with anyone else. What the hell was going on with him? How did he expect me to keep my legs closed for the next six months? I didn't know if I could do it. He said he wasn't going to sleep with Eraina, but how could I trust him to tell me the truth?

After we got off the phone and I saw that bitch walking toward the car, all I saw was red. I put the car in drive and aimed for her ass. If it wasn't for security, I would've tagged her ass big time. I wanted to touch her with that car more than anything. She was very lucky.

Once I swerved the car, I jumped on the highway and rushed home to use the bathroom. Once I got there and plopped down on the cold porcelain commode, I called Tyson to see if we could get together later because I wasn't going to make it for breakfast. It was going to take entirely too long to get ready and be there within the hour. Plus, I had the bubble guts from the cheesecake I ate late night.

"Hey Tray, what's up?" he answered.

"Hey, I'on think I'm gonna make it this morning for breakfast Tyson."

"Aw man, why not?"

"I just don't feel up to it. Maybe we can meet up later this evening or something."

"Uh, why?"

"I just told you I'm not feeling well..."

"But you were fine just a little while ago," he interrupted.

"Yea, that's the thing about pregnancy. Sometimes, I feel great and other times, not so good. I just wanted to know if we could get some dinner later. Or you can come here and we can just talk."

"Well, I'ma keep it real witchu Tray. I already made plans," he stated like it wasn't a big deal to shoot me down. Call it intuition, but from the sound of his voice, I already knew that he had probably made plans with that bitch Eraina.

"You have plans with who Tyson?" I asked as I drummed my nails on the countertop.

"Huh?"

"You can't hear me now? Who do you have plans with? I mean, you just got home!"

"Why do you need to know all that? We ain't together no more Tray!"

"You sound a lil mad cuz I'm asking you a question. All I asked was who you had plans with. And you don't have to keep reminding me that we aren't together anymore! I'm not some little special ed kid or something. I understand shit very clear! The attitude you are displaying just lets me know that you have plans with your other baby mama," I concluded. "Am I right?"

"Tray..."

"Am I right? C'mon, you can tell me the truth Tyson. We both grown," I reminded.

Even though I wanted him to tell me the truth, I was pissed already before he even confirmed what I already knew. He was getting together with that bitch, but he didn't want me to know because he knew I would blow up. Why the hell was he seeing her tonight as opposed to seeing me. He had already been with that bitch for two damn weeks. Whatever Tyson had to say to Eraina, he should've already said it while he was with her on the damn rig for two fucking weeks!

Now he wanted to blow me off to be with her and he thought I was going to be okay with that shit?! No, I wasn't happy about the shit and I let him know right away, not biting my tongue one bit! Not until he cut me off.

"Tray, I need you to calm down..."

"Don't fucking tell me to calm down like I'm some little kid blowing a gasket for no reason Tyson! You just got home after spending two weeks on the water with that bitch! Please explain to me why you aren't spending your first night with me instead of with her!"

"Tray I was gonna take you to breakfast this morning. You're the one who couldn't make it and that's cool. We can just meet up tomorrow. I just don't understand why you have to make such a big deal out of everything?"

"Let me tell you something Tyson. I'm not gonna sit around here and wait for you to decide that I'm a good fucking woman. I know what kind of woman I am, so if you can't appreciate me for what I can bring to the table, maybe someone else will!"

"What's that supposed to mean Tray?"

"It means what you won't do, another nigga will and with no problem! Keep playing with me and I will show you better than I can tell you," I threatened.

"You know what Tray? Just do whatever you wanna do. I'm tired playing these damn games with you. It's sad that I'm trying to be grown about this situation and you're still stuck on some childish bullshit..."

"CHILDISH?!! BULLSHIT?!!"

"Yes, childish bullshit! You asked me a question and I was as honest with you as I could be because I refuse to keep lying to you or Eraina. If we are going to make this relationship work to where we can all be cordial with each other for the sake of our kids, then we have to find a common ground," Tyson explained.

"Whatever! Go on your lil date with your other baby mama, but don't expect me to be sitting here waiting on you!" I grunted before I hung the phone up.

It was 9am in the morning and I had to do something to stay busy so that I wouldn't bug the hell out of Tyson or search for where Eraina lived. Hell, I didn't even know where he lived.

"My life is so messed up!" I cried as I started cleaning my kitchen. Next, I went to the living room, the front closet, the bathroom, my bedroom, my master bathroom, then finally I had my walk-in closet left.

Feeling exhausted, I sat my sweaty ass on the floor in front of the closet. It wasn't that bad, but it needed some rearranging.

Looking at the clock hanging on my bedroom wall, I saw that it was after 4pm and I hadn't eaten anything but a bunch of snacks all day. I was as hungry as a horse right about now.

The thought of a meal made me think about Tyson. He had me fucked up if he thought I was just going to sit here and twiddle my thumbs while he was out on a date with that bitch. He could kick rocks because I was no one's second choice. I was too damn fine to be taking shit from him.

Huffing heavily, I got up and went into my closet to draw out this sexy red dress that still had the tags hanging from it. Yeah, with that bad baby on, I was ready to hit the club.

After I stripped down, I stepped into the shower and washed all the dirt and grime off of my body. Then I applied apple scented lotion to my dampened body before spraying some apple scented body mist. When I was done, I grabbed the dress that was laying on my bed and struggled to get it over my head.

I started to wonder if my head had gotten bigger since I found out I was pregnant. I had an even harder time pulling that dress down over my hips! Once I finally got it on and properly positioned, I thought I looked pretty damn good.

The dress did fit a bit snug, but since I wasn't showing too much yet, I could get by with wearing this. My belly was just starting to show, so it looked like I had a small FUPA sitting over my kitty and nothing else.

Digging on the top of my shoe rack, I grabbed some nude heels to match the nude, red and black handbag that I had already been carrying. After snatching that up along with my keys, I headed out the door. Sliding in my car, I hit the engine button as I held the brake down then backed out of the driveway.

As I listened to music, I rode around with no place to go. I didn't know what I was going to do, but Tyson had the wrong one if he thought I wasn't going to go out in search of something or someone. Yea, maybe I was reverting back to my old ways, but he left me no choice.

After swinging through a drive-thru to put something on my stomach, I hit up a popular club on the northside and paid the cover charge to get in. Once inside, I noticed that the club was jumping. It had been a long time since I had hit the club and I was going to enjoy myself tonight. Yes, it was true that the last time I was out, I got lit with all the alcohol I had consumed. This time, with the pregnancy and all, drinking wasn't an option for me.

Where was it written that I had to drink in order to have fun. I did walk up to the bar and order a glass of wine though. I had read somewhere that a glass of wine wouldn't endanger the baby and it would ease my mind. I was definitely looking for something to relax me. I took my wine and headed to a table closest to the dance floor.

Once I got comfortable in my seat, I started bobbing my head and tapping my foot to the sounds of Jacquees. Slowly, I began to let the rhythm on the music relax me. It didn't matter that I was all alone or had a million and one problems at that moment. No, no! I was in my own little world and no one could spoil it for me. It could only get better.

"Hey beautiful! Long time no see!" I heard a familiar voice whisper from behind me.

Slowly turning around in my seat, I came face to face with one of my regular clients, Donavan with his handsome rich self! A smile quickly spread over my face as I allowed him to kiss my hand and take a seat next to me.

"Damn, I've been missing you girl!" he laughed wrapping his arm around my waist. "You got time for me tonight?"

Dollars and dick sounded pretty good on the menu for that night. Hell, Tyson wasn't giving me none and my stash was getting low. What, oh, what, was a woman to do?

Before I could make a decision, I felt an eerie shadow hovering over me. Looking up at the enemy, I began scooting back in my chair.

"Hell nah, she don't got time for you! She's meeting me here!" Jose intervened with a scowl while lifting his jacket to reveal the butt of a gun.

My knees weakened as Donavan got up from the table with his hands raised. Was that nigga really about to just walk away and leave me alone with this crazy motherfucker, Jose?! Was he just going to get himself out of danger and leave me to get killed?!

"Wait! Donavan! I thought you said..."

"No, that's alright. I'll catch up with you later," he sang out as he darted from the table. I could've just chased his ass down and jumped on his damn back for leaving me like that! He was lucky that I was pregnant!

"I'on know why you were just sitting here wasting your time with that funny looking nigga when I told you that I was gonna take care of you Trashelle!" Jose whined as he took the seat Donavan skedaddled out of before scooting closer to me. "Let's get outta here baby."

"I'm not going anywhere with you Jose! If you're gonna kill me, you're gonna have to do it right here in front of all these people!" I hissed trying to scare him, but it did no good. This man still pulled it out and cocked the hammer.

My eyes bucked and knees buckled as he drew me upward to my feet. I wanted so badly to scream, but nothing came out. All I could do was cry, tremble and pray that someone would help me.

"Stop! Why are you doing this?" I cried trying to pry his hands off my arm as he dragged me out the front door of the club. Right by the damn security guard too!

When I saw that muthafucka wink at Jose, my stomach dropped, and I was ready to pass the fuck out! I literally had no one to help me!

Maybe if I could get to my cell that was in the outside pocket of my handbag. If I could, then I would be able to quick dial Tyson. Sure, he unblocked me, but the problem was, would he even answer?

Chapter Fifteen

Tyson

Tray was really tripping if she thought that I was supposed to change my schedule just because she was running late for breakfast. When I invited her to breakfast, she should've just told me that she had to do something else, but instead she wanted to call me and try to run shit. No buddy! Those days of running me were over and she would soon find that out.

After Tray called me acting a damn nut, I really wanted to block her again, but I didn't. Only because I promised that I wouldn't and to show that I was a man of my word, I was going to try my hardest to stick to it.

With my body aching, I got off the shuttle with Johnson and went down the ramp before we parted ways. Throwing my hand up, I bid him farewell and told him that I would see him at the gym soon.

"Damn, those two weeks kicked my ass!" I huffed as I got in my vehicle to leave the docks. I couldn't wait to get back to my new house and jump in the shower.

Soon as I made it there 20 minutes later, I washed my ass then changed clothes. I got on my Postmates app and ordered some IHOP since Tray canceled breakfast. It came in no time too.

After I messed that meal up, I needed a nap. Laying across my bed, I dozed off and didn't wake up until 4pm. That was just enough time to get myself together before I had to pick Eraina up for our dinner date to discuss things. I called myself creating a calendar with all of her and Tray's appointments because I planned on going to as many as I could.

"Let me get my ass up!"

Since we were going to a nice restaurant, I got out the bed and went to the closet to find some jeans and a button-down collared shirt. To complete the outfit, I drew out one of my new blazers. Had a nigga looking real fly.

"Damn, I almost forgot how fine I was when I cleaned up!" I laughed at myself as I clowned in the mirror. Had me taking a few selfies. That was how much I was feeling myself.

Silently wondering to myself, I thought about what Eraina was going to wear. Since she took out her braids, she had been sporting this tired old ponytail. I prayed she was going to do something with that shit and didn't bring her ass out embarrassing the both of us!

Calling her up once I was ready, she picked up on the first ring sounding all excited. She had me laughing at her ass too.

"Girl, what's wrong with you?" I teased.

"Nothing Tyson!"

"It's something Eraina. What is it?" I pressed.

"It's just that it feels like our first date or something." She giggled. "Are you gonna open my door and everything when you pick me up?"

"Yeah, I can do that, but this ain't like a date-date, Eraina," I reminded without trying to hurt her feelings.

"Close enough for me! You're picking me up, paying for it and you're gonna open my door!" she screamed. "I can't wait!"

"Are you ready?"

"I've been ready for the last 20 minutes!" she admitted shamelessly. "I can't even sit still! I haven't been this excited since prom night!"

"You crazy girl!" I laughed. "I'll be pulling up in about five minutes."

"I'll be outside!" She giggled before hanging up.

All I could do was shake my head and smile. Eraina was a nice chick and I wished her the best. Even though she wasn't the woman for me, I was willing to respect her as the mother of my child and that was going to be important for him or her to see.

As I thought about what it took to be a great parent, I started thinking of other ways to be involved with my baby mamas' pregnancies without having relations with either women. It would be hard, but that was one of my goals.

"Damn! God you tryna test me already!" I grunted as I pulled up in front of Eraina's apartment. She was standing out front in a form fitting black dress that clung to her body like a latex glove. I'm saying, it was gripping every curve and I couldn't take my eyes off her. Shit, she even had her hair done! It was hanging down and blowing in the wind. Looking like a plus sized model!

Drawing my ride up in the stall next to her car, I got out, walked around to the other side and opened her door before I greeted her. "Look at you. looking all nice and shit!" I teased.

"Thank you, Tyson!" Eraina blushed as she gently climbed in the passenger seat and buckled up.

When I got in, she must've thanked me ten more times before we made it to the restaurant. After parking, I walked around and let Eraina out before escorting her inside the fine establishment.

We were immediately seated and jumped right into a conversation on our parenting ideas. The more ideas Eraina shared, the more intrigued I became with having these two kids. She had me thinking that I could really be a great father.

"I hope so!"

"You will Tyson! Just watch!" Eraina smiled as she sipped on her lemon water while I downed my second shot of Jack Daniels.

Before I knew it, I was on my third, then fourth... then I was really feeling it. I should've known better when I had to drive. Eraina called me on the shit soon as I stood up and stumbled a bit.

"I guess I'm gonna have to drive huh?" she smiled and took the keys. "You can either come to my house and sleep it off, or when we get there, I can get you an Uber and you come get your ride tomorrow."

Just as I opened my mouth to answer, my cell started ringing. It was Tray, but I wasn't in the mood to deal with her when I was with Eraina. I was going to just wait and call her back, but she called four or five more times in a row. Something wasn't right.

"Hello?"

"Tyson!" Tray screamed. "Jose! Jose has me!"

"Where are you?!" I asked sobering up as much as possible.

As Tray gave me the address to some cheesy club on the southside, I put it in the GPS and had Eraina shoot over there. I mean, what else could I do? I wasn't about to take her all the way home when Tray was in danger. No, she had to go too, and I didn't give a damn who didn't like it.

"What happened Tyson? Where are we going?" Eraina asked with a worried expression.

"Tray is in some trouble and I gotta go see what's up," I explained.

"Okay, let me hurry up!" Eraina shouted as she floored it, surprising the shit out of me. I could've sworn she hated Tray!

Either way and whatever the reason was, I was thankful that Eraina was willing to understand. To make sure, I thanked her and told her that if it was her, I would do the same thing.

"I know you would Tyson. That's one of the things I love about you," Eraina confessed without looking at me.

"Thanks," I whispered as we hit the corner damn near on two wheels.

As I held on for dear life, Eraina recklessly got us to the destination. I had to hold in the vomit that was threatening to come up. Thankfully I had a bottle of water in the car to sip on to keep it down.

"Where is she?" I huffed as we rolled up in the driveway leading to the parking lot.

"Look Tyson! Is that her over there?" Eraina yelled pointing over to someone balled up in the dark corner of the lot.

"Yeah, I think it is!"

When Eraina pulled over, she told me that she would stay in the car while I went to check on her. "I gotta call Nessa and check in with her anyhow."

"Okay," I replied as I got out and walked over to Tray. "Tray!"

"Tyson?!" she hollered as she looked up at me with bloodshot eyes.

"What happened?" I gasped as I helped her to her feet only to see her slinky dressed ripped halfway off her body. I couldn't even get mad that she was pregnant and out at a club after I saw the bruises all over her.

"Jose! It was Jose!"

"Did you call the cops?"

"No! I called you!" Tray cried as I helped her to the backseat of my vehicle.

Tray was cool until she got in and saw Eraina behind the wheel of my whip. Beat up and bruised or not, this chick went way off. I'm talking all the way to the left and snatched Eraina by the hair from behind.

"You brought this bitch with you to pick me up Tyson?! And you got her driving your car too?!" Tray cried smelling like alcohol. I could've just knocked her ass out, but I couldn't because I had to pry her hands out of Eraina's hair.

"Stop Tray! Let go!" I shouted until I got Tray's fingers out of Eraina's hair.

"Are you fucking kidding me right now Tray?" I asked angrily. "Eraina, drive us to the nearest hospital!"

"I'm not going anywhere with that bitch!" Tray fussed.

"You ain't got a damn choice! You were attacked and you need to get checked out!" I said.

"Let me out of this damn car!" she fumed.

"Eraina DRIVE TO THE NEAREST HOSPITAL!!" I yelled as I held Tray back.

"You got me fucked up Tyson! I can't believe you thought this shit was okay!" Tray continued.

"You knew I had plans! When you called for help, I was still with her! What did you expect me to do?" I asked.

"Well, I sure didn't expect for you to bring her with you! This ain't her business!" Tray continued fussing with me as I held her back from striking Eraina again.

However, I was only holding her arms and hands. When she thrust her foot out and kicked the driver's seat of my car hard, I couldn't believe it. Like damn!

I just didn't understand why Tray hated Eraina so much when everything going on between them was my fault. It was my fault we were all in this fucked up situation that was forcing us to get along for the sake of my kids. Tray was going to have to learn some self- control because she couldn't keep acting out like that every time that she was pissed about something.

"Right here!" I hollered gesturing Eraina to veer the car into the next entrance.

Immediately, Eraina pulled into the hospital parking lot and hurried over to the emergency department. She blew the horn when we drove up to the double doors and a nurse ran right out with a wheelchair.

As the timid white red headed nurse opened the back door, she saw me holding Tray's hands. Right away she thought the wrong shit.

"Oh my God!" this bitch screeched assuming that I was abusing Trashelle. "Get off of her!"

"Wait! I didn't do this to her!" I replied defensively as I released Tray.

Soon as I did, she promptly struck Eraina behind the head before sliding out of the back seat and plopping down into the wheelchair. As Tray slumped into the wheelchair, a line of blood trickled down her leg from beneath her dress. She looked up at me with fright in her eyes.

This was exactly what I was trying to avoid. Now, her foolish ass was looking at me like I had did something wrong. All I could do was shake my fucking head as the nurse wheeled her inside.

I turned to look at Eraina only to see tears creeping from the corners of her eyes. "I'll go park the car," she said. "You go be with her!"

WOW! I can't believe this shit is happening! We were just talking about future plans and now this?!

Nodding my head at Eraina, I closed the back door and headed inside the hospital. I followed behind the nurse as she wheeled Tray through the doors leading to the exam rooms. At this point, all I could do was pray.

Chapter Sixteen

Nessa

"Eraina! What the hell is going on?" I screamed into the phone as I heard my best friend yelling like someone was hurting her.

Ready to jump in my car and race to her rescue, I listened as shit calmed down. A few minutes later, she spoke into the phone again.

"What the hell?" I asked.

"Girl you are not going to believe this shit!"

"Try me bitch!"

"Okay, so Tyson picked me up for our dinner, right? We had a good talk and I really felt as if we had made some progress. Why when we were leaving the restaurant, Trashelle called him?"

"What? What the hell did that bitch want?" I asked.

"I don't know girl. She wanted Tyson to come get her!"

"Get her from where?"

"The club girl! That bitch was at the club! Pregnant and all Nessa!" Eraina blurted out with a loud laugh.

"Girl I know you fuckin' lyin'!"

"No, I'm not. Hell, I couldn't make this shit up if I wanted to!"

"So, did he go to the club to get her?"

"We both did! I was driving because Tyson had thrown back a few too many. We found that ho' lying on the ground, her dress was ripped and full of blood. She looked like that dope fiend on that *Holiday Heart* movie." She busted out laughing again and so did I.

"Girl you are a fool!" I clowned. "What happened to that bitch?"

"Girl, I have no idea. I think she was attacked or something," Eraina answered.

"What happened after that?"

"So, anyway, Tyson told me to drive to the hospital and do you know that bitch started attacking me for being in the car?"

"Damn!"

"Yea, she was hitting me from behind while Tyson was trying to hold her back! I couldn't believe that shit!" Eraina said. "I wanted to beat the hell out of that bitch for putting her hands on me!"

"I bet you did!"

"But she got her karma served to her though."

"Why girl, what happened?"

"Girl as soon as she got her ass in the wheelchair, she started bleeding!" Eraina explained.

"What you mean bleeding? Didn't you already say her dress was ripped and bloody?" I asked.

"Yea, I did say that, but she started bleeding between her legs girl," Eraina explained, going into detail.

"Oh wow! So, you saying she had a miscarriage?"

"I don't know what the hell going on with her. I stayed to park the car while Tyson went inside with her..."

"Bitch you still outside? You need to be in there so you can find out what's going on!" I said.

"Yea, I guess you're right," she said.

"Yea. Call or text me as soon as you know something!"

"Okay, I will. Talk to you soon."

We ended the call and I made myself comfortable while laughing at Eraina's situation. That was some crazy shit!

I hoped and prayed that bitch Trashelle would lose her baby for my homegirl Eraina's sake. That girl didn't deserve to have a baby and apparently, she didn't give a damn either way. I mean, she was out there clubbing while pregnant.

What kind of shit was that? A pregnant woman did not belong in the club. She had no business being there.

"It's always the careless ratchet ones that wind up lucky enough to get knocked up." I huffed.

I wished I could trade places with Trashelle. I wished I was the one who was pregnant instead of her. At least I wouldn't be gyrating all in the club like some unpregnant, irresponsible chick.

I couldn't understand why women who were pregnant cared more about themselves than the babies they were carrying. That shit made absolutely no sense to me. While I was sitting here wanting a baby, Trashelle was... scratch that because she might be having a miscarriage.

Again, I prayed that was what was happening. At least one of us could be happy. If Trashelle lost that baby, Eraina could have her man and their baby, making them a happy family.

As for me, the more I thought about it... maybe it was good that I didn't get pregnant by Byron because I was happy that I finally left his ass alone. He was not the man for me. I didn't know what was going on with him and his wife, but I was happy to not be a part of it anymore.

Besides, I had been keeping my time occupied with better things. For starters, I had been seeing someone special for about two weeks now. His name was Arturo and I had met him at the nail shop of all places. Arturo was getting a pedicure with his sister. He happened to be sitting next to me and somehow the two of us struck up a conversation. While he got the deluxe package for his feet, I got the one that included both a manicure and pedicure. That was enough time for us to get to know one another.

Since Arturo was there before I arrived, he finished before my manicure even began. Don't think that I let him get away without us exchanging numbers though. Nah, a bitch was on that opportunity and wasn't about to let it slip through my fingers without exploring it in several different ways.

Licking my lips with thoughts of me and Arturo's first connection, I sat on my sofa and smiled. As I wiggled around to get comfortable, my phone rang.

It startled me when I looked at it and saw that it was Byron. He hadn't called in so long that I thought I was truly rid of him.

"I don't know why the hell he's calling me! I ain't got shit to tell his ass. Fuck you Byron!" I yelled as if he could hear me on a call that I hadn't even connected and didn't plan on it either.

"I'm not answering in!"

It stopped ringing and I sighed heavily feeling relieved until it started ringing once again. "Ugh!"

As I glanced down at the screen, I would be lying if I said that I didn't wonder what he wanted. Yes, I was tempted, but I wasn't budging, and I didn't care enough to pick up the phone to find out.

"I got something for yo ass!" I whispered waiting for my cell to stop ringing.

Soon as it did, I rushed to put Byron's number on my block list. I didn't have shit to say to him at all. He probably just wanted to bother me about getting rid of those text messages. I wasn't about to do that. It was my leverage to keep his shady ass in line.

"Not again!" I huffed when my phone started ringing again. I almost picked up and screamed into it until I saw that it was Arturo calling.

"Hello."

"Hola Mami," Arturo greeted in his rich Spanish accent.

"Hey, what's going on?" I asked.

"I just was thinking about you."

"Oh wow! Thinking about me already huh?"

The two of us stayed on the phone for about two hours when my phone started beeping with another call. "Hold up. Let me see who that is?"

I clicked over to the other line and it was Eraina. "Hold up girl. Let me hang the other line up," I said before clicking over to my previous call. "Arturo can I talk to you tomorrow? That's my friend on the other line and she really needs to talk to me."

"Yea, sure Mami. I will call you tomorrow," he said. "Sleep tight."

"Thanks, you too."

The second I switched calls, Eraina started asking questions.

"Who were you on the phone with at almost midnight?"

"Forget that! What's going on at the hospital? Is that bitch still pregnant?"

"Nope! She lost the baby," Eraina sang happily.

"Hallelujah!" I rejoiced as I stood up and did the holy dance.

"Girl stop!" she hissed, even though I knew she was happy.

"Girl bye! Don't act like you ain't happy that bitch lost her baby! Did you forget she tried to run over you earlier?" I asked.

"Of course, I didn't forget. I'm not saying I'm not happy either. I guess I just feel bad for her."

"Bad for her? Bitch please! That bitch was trying to fuck up your relationship with Tyson since the day she found out. She knows your pregnant but still tried to run you over earlier at the dock! She deserves every fucking thing she gets!" I fussed. "You can't treat people any kind of way and think nothing will happen to you! God doesn't like ugly baby!"

"I know but damn!" Eraina whined like a damn fool. "I can't imagine how I would feel if I lost my baby, so I can't possibly imagine how she feels."

"Fuck that bitch! You won Eraina! YOU WON!!" I shrieked happily.

"Won what Nessa?"

"You won Tyson sis! You best believe that now that you're giving him his first and only child, he is going to want to be there for you! Now he doesn't have to split his time between you and her cuz she ain't pregnant no mo'! Shit you need to be happier about that!" I said, not understanding why she wasn't rejoicing happily like me.

I can't possibly be the only one that's happy for her!

"You better stop feeling sorry for that bitch because you know if it would've been you who had lost your baby, she wouldn't be sitting there talking mad shit about you Eraina," I assured my best friend.

"You're right. You just had to see how devastated she was."

"FUCK HER!!" I fumed.

"Well, I'll talk to you later. I just got home and I need to take a shower. I just feel icky!"

"Yea, I'll call you tomorrow."

We ended the call and I rolled over and went to sleep. I didn't know where Eraina was going with those feelings, but she'd better seize that opportunity to get her man. The way I saw it, the better woman won.

Chapter Twenty-One

Trashelle

Never in my life did I think that one night at the club was going to leave me in the hospital without my baby. I had gone to the club just to spite Tyson for not giving me the attention he was giving Eraina. That shit hurt my feelings, but knowing that Jose was still out there, I should've kept my black ass at home where I was. At least there, I had my neighbors looking out for me. Here, no one gave two shits what was happening to the next person.

Why the hell did I have to be so stupid?

Running into Jose at the club wasn't part of the plan. Then to have him pull me outside like I was his property and not get any help from security. The way dude looked at him, I could tell that they knew each other. Damn, was I in enemy territory or something? I was definitely slipping with that stupid move.

Drawing me in the dark corner of the lot, I balled up and continued to urge him to stop hitting me. Once outside, Jose started hitting me.

Then, thinking that someone was going to help me when Jose started hitting me and making me scream was obviously the wrong assumption. Sadly, folks were walking right on by us without even asking if I was okay. I was so damn scared that I even told Jose that I was pregnant just to get him to stop.

"Please Jose! Don't hurt me! I'M PREGNANT!!" I screamed repeating myself.

"You're what? You're having some other dude's baby?" Jose asked.

"I'm sorry Jose! Please don't hurt me! DON'T HURT MY BABY!!"

Hearing that I was pregnant didn't help my case at all. And begging this fool not to hurt my baby had fallen on deaf ears. All Jose heard was that I was having another man's baby. That was when his blows started connecting with my stomach. I tried my best to keep him from hurting my baby, but he was ruthless. If it hadn't been for a couple of partygoers, Jose probably would've killed me.

When those dudes yelled at him, for some reason he took off. I expected him to wave his gun at them and continue beating me, but he didn't. I guess he felt the deed was done, so his job was done. After he left, I could barely move. The two dudes came to check on me, but they were laughing so hard that they walked away. I wanted to call the cops, but I needed to call someone else first.

I could barely make the call to Tyson, but I managed to locate his number and ask for help. I huddled up in the corner praying that Tyson would come soon.

Man, when I said that I was happy when I saw Tyson's car pull up... I was now releasing tears of joy to know that he actually came for me.

Yea, all that went to shit when I got in and saw that Tyson wasn't by himself. He had the nerve to have Eraina's bitch ass with him.

Why would he do that? How could he disrespect me by bringing that bitch when he knew he was coming to get me? I didn't know where the strength came from, but I grabbed Eraina from behind and started hitting her upside her head. I think I struck her twice before Tyson held my hands.

"Are you crazy? Are you trying to lose the fucking baby?" Tyson asked angrily.

"Why the fuck would you bring her when you knew you were coming to get me? What the fuck kinda shit is that? You don't have no fucking respect for me at all!" I yelled.

"No respect for you? You don't have respect for your damn self! Do you see what the hell you got on? You're pregnant and you got your fucking ass all out! You smell like you been drinking and shit! What the fuck Tray?" he continued fussing at me like I was his kid or something.

I was in a lot of pain, so the last thing I needed was for Tyson to be going off on me in front of that bitch! I was furious but I couldn't do shit about it. The only thing I could do was wait to get to the hospital and get checked out. All the while, I prayed that I wouldn't lose my baby.

As we arrived and a nurse rushed out with a wheelchair, Tyson was right there with me. Just his presence alone made me think everything was going to be okay.

"What's going on?" a nurse on duty asked before taking me into a room.

She took one look at me and I saw a look of sadness across her face. "Were you in a fight?" she asked.

"You could say that. Please check on my baby!" I cried as I held on to my sore stomach.

"You're pregnant?"

"Yes, 11 and a half weeks," I responded, hoping that was still the case.

"I'll be right back."

She left and returned a short time later with the doctor. After a quick examination, he ordered an ultrasound. The nurse left the room in a haste and returned with the machine. She wheeled the ultrasound machine next to the bed and typed in the necessary information. After I confirmed my name and date of birth, she began to roll the wand over my belly.

As she searched for my little one on the screen, I winced in pain. My stomach was bruised from the punches that I sustained from Jose's beating. As I stared at the screen, I squinted in an effort to see my baby's tiny heart beating. I needed something to show me that he or she was still alive in my womb. But it didn't take long for me to realize that there was no more baby. In a horrifying daze, I began panicking.

"Where's my baby's heart? Why isn't it beating on the monitor?" I asked nervously, even though I had a feeling the news was bad.

Without even responding to any of my questions, the nurse excused herself. I looked at Tyson with tears in my eyes. I was still holding on to hope when the doctor came in followed by the nurse.

Taking a seat on the nearby swivel stool, the physician grabbed the wand and looked at the monitor while rubbing the wand on my belly. He studied the screen so hard that he had creases in his forehead.

After several minutes, he finally cleaned off the wand and my stomach before turning to look at me. "I am so sorry..."

"No please... don't tell me that!" I begged shaking my head from side to side.

"I wish I had some better news for you, but unfortunately, I can't find a heartbeat."

"NOOOOOO!"

"I'm afraid you've suffered a miscarriage."

"It's a mistake doc! It has to be!"

"I'm afraid there's no mistake. I'm so sorry," he apologized.

"Wow!" Tyson managed to get out.

"The next step is to perform a D and C to remove the remaining tissues from your uterus..."

The doctor was still talking but I had drifted off after he told me that my baby was gone. I couldn't believe that just this morning I was thinking about my future with Tyson as parents to our child and now, I was lying in a hospital bed crying over the loss of our baby. I wanted to be held by Tyson but the way he was looking at me, I could tell that comforting me was the last thing he wanted to do.

Waiting for the doctor to leave the room to go get what he needed to perform the necessary procedure, I whispered, "I'm sorry," as tears continued to rain down my cheeks.

"I know Tray. I know."

I was sure he was thinking if I would've stayed home none of this shit would be happening. I knew he was thinking it because I was thinking it too. I had lost my precious little baby because I wanted to prove a point to Tyson and now, I was laying there sulking. No baby. No man, and no one to blame but my damn self.

Then it hit me... Eraina was still pregnant!

Oh God! Why did you take my baby away? How come she gets to keep hers and I didn't get to keep mine? What did I do wrong?

What a stupid question. I knew exactly what I had done wrong. Before I even left the house, I knew that Jose was still out there. However, he was the furthest thing from my mind. All I wanted was to get back at Tyson for his lack of attention. So, instead of staying home, I went out like a damn fool.

I swore to myself in that moment that if I ever saw Jose again, I would kill him on sight. He didn't deserve to be living after what he had done to me and my precious baby.

Interrupting my sad mental rant, the doctor returned and asked Tyson to step out so he could perform the procedure. While I wanted him to stay, the doctor felt since we weren't married it was best if he stepped out.

Instead of fussing, Tyson said that he had some business to take care of anyway, so he didn't mind. I bet that business had a lot to do with that bitch Eraina. With that chick on my mind, I could barely stay still as I laid on the bed with my legs in stirrups. Clinching up, I tried my best to relax as the doctor did what he had to do.

Once he was done, he sent me to radiology for x-rays only because I revealed that Jose beat me up. After finding that out, I couldn't stop him from calling the cops to make a report, nor did I want to.

After everything Jose had put me through tonight, he deserved to be locked up like the monster that he was.

So, now, there was an all- points bulletin out on Jose's ass. He had better hope that they found him before I did. He had stepped up to me for the last damn time. If it wasn't Jose, it was Eraina! As far as I was concerned, they both had to go!

If my baby is gone, hers should be too!

*****

Crying my eyes out as I repeated the story to the police a couple of hours later, I noticed that Tyson still hadn't come back. I couldn't wait to call him to see where the hell he was as soon as the cops left. I mean damn! Was that bitch Eraina that damn important? I was the one who lost my baby! How the hell would I ever recover from that shit?

"Hello?!" I screeched.

"What's wrong now, Tray?"

"Duh! I lost our baby Tyson! Why aren't you here with me?!"

"The nurse said she would come get me when you were done. She ain't come yet..."

"I'm done and I'm ready to go Tyson!"

"I'm coming Tray! Damn! I'm on my way!"

"And not with that bitch Eraina either! I don't need to see her to remind me that she's still having your baby and I'm not!" I cried not able to hold it in.

"I just dropped her off Tray, so you don't have to worry about seeing her."

Hanging up in Tyson's face, I bawled my eyes out until he showed up 20 minutes later. No lie, I was mad as all outdoors until he came into the room with flowers in his hand.

"You ready?"

"Yea, they called in my prescriptions and I can pick them up on the way home. My car is still at the..."

"I already called and had it towed to your house Tray. They sent me a text about an hour ago to let me know it was there," Tyson explained. "Let's just get you out of this depressing ass place."

Helping me off the hospital bed, Tyson helped the nurse put me in the wheelchair to get wheeled to the exit. He then grabbed my bag with my personal belongings in it and followed out front where his truck was illegally parked.

As the rising sun beamed in my face, Tyson assisted me in his vehicle, buckled me up then went to hop in behind the steering wheel.

"You cool?" he asked before pulling off.

"No, Tyson, I'm not cool! How can I be cool when I lost our baby?" I sniffled as I turned my head to look out the window in an effort to mask my tears. Tyson didn't reply. He just kept quiet and stared ahead as he drove me home.

Driving along the main road, the first stop Tyson made was at the pharmacy to pick up my meds. Secondly, we stopped by a drive-thru to get me some tacos and Mexi-fries. Finally, we arrived at my house.

After Tyson made sure I ate and took my meds, he tucked me in and grabbed his keys. "I'll check on you in the morning Tray."

"What? You aren't going to stay with me?" I asked almost in tears all over again.

How could he even think about leaving me after what I had been through? For him to not even offer to stay had me feeling abandoned when he hadn't left the room yet. Was he leaving me to go be with his baby mama? What was so important that he couldn't be here with me tonight when I needed him the most?

"Well, I wasn't planning to..."

"Well, can you plan to now? I've been through a traumatic experience Tyson. I don't wanna have nightmares and wake up by myself. Would it kill you to stay with me this one night?" I begged, hoping that he would have a heart and stay with me.

Setting his keys on my nightstand, Tyson kicked off his shoes and laid on top of my comforter. Sure, I wanted him in between the sheets next to me, but I wasn't about to sweat him. He should've wanted to be with me to comfort me. Why was he being so cold?

As these hurtful thoughts haunted my mind, I tried to cuddle up with Tyson. Unfortunately, the closest I got was to lay my head on his chest.

Accepting what little affection that was offered to me, I closed my eyes and let the meds take control. In no time, I was knocked out. That was exactly why I didn't notice when Tyson crept out.

All I know is when I woke up at 5am, that nigga was gone, and I was alone once again...

Chapter Twenty-Two

Tyson

So much happened so fast. Just when I started to get used to the idea of having two kids, one was carelessly ripped away. Never did I think that it would bother me like it did, but the more I thought about how Tray put herself out there like that, the more I believed she knew what she was doing.

No, I didn't want to blame Tray, but damn! It was hard not to. I mean, it was technically her fucking fault. Why didn't she just stay her fucking ass at home and act like the pregnant woman she was. Why did she have to go out to some fucking nightclub in her condition in the first place? That was dumb and irresponsible on her part.

Then she had the nerve to talk shit to me because she lost the baby. I had nothing to do with the decision she made to go strut her ass in some fucking club.

I was glad that Eraina was there because I didn't know how I would've reacted if I had to face Tray alone. I wanted to yell at her and cuss her ass out, but what good would that have done? What would that have solved? It wouldn't have made a damn bit of difference, and it wouldn't have brought the baby back. In the bible it said to accept the things we cannot change, so that was what I did.

A Month Later...

Over this past month, Eraina had done everything she could to be helpful. She had helped me through the situation with Tray and had even got a job with another company before her stomach got too big just like she promised. All that made it easier for me to focus on my job and it was a getaway as well.

Too bad those 14 days flew by fast. Too quickly for me and before I knew it, I was arriving back at the docks. As I walked down the ramp, I heard someone calling my name.

"Tyson!" Eraina sang out as she headed towards me.

Ever since that night I took her to dinner, she had been going out of her way to look nice. Even coming from her hitch, she had her hair up in a curly ponytail and was wearing a black and white hip-hugging jogging suit with a pair of fresh white sneakers to match.

"So, I see you made it through your first hitch huh?" I teased.

"I've been telling you all week that I was! It's easy and I'm almost glad I changed jobs," Eraina giggled. "Thanks for all the texts though Tyson. Some of them really got me through. I appreciate you."

"No problem."

"So, how is Trashelle doing?" Eraina asked, which really shocked the shit out of me and threw me off. Since when did she start caring about Tray?

"Good, I guess... I haven't really talked to her..."

"Well, I wasn't gonna bring it up..."

"You wasn't gonna bring what up Eraina?" I questioned with a raised brow knowing it was about to be some shit.

"Well, I didn't mention it before because I thought it would stop..."

"What would stop Eraina?" I pressed. "What are you saying?"

"I'm saying that Trashelle has been sending me threatening messages..."

"What kind of messages?" I huffed heavily not believing what Eraina was telling me.

"She keeps threatening me and our baby Tyson. I'm sure it's harmless, but she needs some help. Maybe, someone to talk to," Eraina suggested with a look of concern.

"She's threatening you how?" I asked wanting some type of clarification.

"Look," she said as she drew her cell out and began scrolling through her messages. "Start from here."

My eyes almost bucked out of my damn head as I read how Tray told Eraina that she would shoot her in the stomach on sight! She even said she would beat the shit out Eraina until she lost the baby. She blamed Eraina for her unhappiness and even went as far as blaming Eraina for her losing the baby.

It was just a bunch of crazy shit. Tray had said some shit that I would have never expected her to say. It was totally out of her character which led me to believe that maybe Tray did need some type of counseling.

"Damn Eraina! Why are you just now telling me this?! This shit has been going on ever since the morning Tray got out of the hospital!"

"Yea, I didn't tell you because one, I thought she would stop. I just figured she was grieving the loss of her baby and taking it out on me. I figured it was harmless..."

"You should've told me!" I said worrying about Tray. I had to go and check on her.

"I'm sorry Tyson. I thought it was nothing until that last message. I don't know what Trashelle is thinking, but she needs some help."

"Yea, you're right Eraina and I'm about to go check on her before I go home."

"Okay, that's good," she said with a weak smile. "Please tell her I'm praying for her, but if she keeps messaging me stuff like that, I'm going to get a restraining order..."

"A RESTRAINING ORDER?!!"

"Yea, those are some serious threats Tyson and she's obviously being irrational. I mean, she's blaming me because she lost the baby. How was that my fault?"

"I don't know what she was thinking, but it wasn't your fault..."

"You don't have to tell me that! I know it wasn't my fault, but the fact that she blames me let me know that something ain't right," Eraina huffed and smirked.

"Well, like I said, I'm gonna go check on her."

"Well, let me know how it goes and don't forget my doctor's appointment in the morning! I'm ready to prove to you that I'm having a boy! You still don't wanna bet on it?"

"No, because I'm hoping it's a boy too, but either way is cool. You just take care of yourself," I urged before waving goodbye. I needed to hurry to my truck so that I could call Tray up.

Feeling bad that I went against my word and blocked her number, I shook my head as I pressed the green icon to send the call. To my surprise, Tray answered on the first ring.

"Oh, now you wanna call me Tyson?! Now you wanna check on me?!" she snarled. "You've been gone for two whole weeks, 14 damn days! Not to mention I haven't heard from your fucking ass since I lost the baby, but now you wanna call!"

"You at home?"

"Yea, I'm here but what the fuck that gotta do with you?!" she asked in a slurred tone. Yea, she sounded like she had been drinking all damn day.

"I'm coming over there, that's why!"

"Oh, no! Don't you bring yo ass over here now after you left me hanging for fucking weeks! You must be out yo damn mind!"

"I said what I said, and I said I'm coming over there! I got my key, so I'm gonna let myself in."

"Why the hell you still got the key to my damn house? You don't live here no more! Besides, you don't give a fuck about me Tyson! I lost our baby a month ago and you're just now reaching out to me?!"

"That's my fault, but you ain't the only one that lost a baby Tray. Anyway, we'll talk about that when I get over there. This isn't a conversation we should be having over the line. We need to be face to face."

"Why you wanna talk now Tyson? Shouldn't you be with Eraina? She's the one that's still pregnant with your bastard child! Go take your ass over to her house!"

"I'm almost there, Tray. I'm turning by the Shell gas station now."

"Why Tyson?" she cried. "Why did you leave me all alone?"

No matter what I said, Tray cried harder and harder. Of course, I felt bad for her, but I didn't know how to handle no shit like that.

"Stop tripping and open the door Tray. I'm pulling up now."

"You got the key, remember?!" she screamed.

Hopping out my truck, I ran up to the front door and unlocked all three bolts that Tray had installed since the first incident with that nigga Jose. All that shit he had done to her and he was still running around free. I didn't understand the justice system out here.

But from what Tray told me, that fool had ties to law enforcement. Apparently, some of his family members worked for the Houston Police Department. A couple of them were even lawyers and one was a judge. That nigga had everybody taking his side.

None of that should've mattered. He violated Tray on more than one occasion and made her lose our baby. Hell, that shit right there was murder!

That nigga should've been locked the hell up in somebody's prison!

"Tray?!" I yelled out as I entered the house and was greeted by the stench of old food and weed.

The house was a mess. The tables, floors and sofa were covered with takeout containers and bags. There were at least three ashtrays laying around overflowing with cigarette butts and blunt roaches.

On the floor, I counted at least ten empty fifths of Jack Daniels and a couple of Crown Royal bottles as well. I couldn't believe the disaster. Her place was fucked up, so that meant she was fucked up.

Climbing over the trash, I yelled out for Tray again as I headed towards the master bedroom. "Tray!"

"What the hell do you want?!" she hollered from the bathroom. I could tell she had tried to hurry to wash her ass before I got here. Too bad she didn't get to her hair. That shit looked like she had stuck her finger in the light socket.

"I came by to check on you and I'm glad I did too! Yo house is fucked up Tray! What's going on with you?"

"I lost our baby Tyson!" she screamed looking like she was possessed and shit. "Don't you fucking care? Did you even shed a fucking tear for our baby Tyson?!"

This bitch was going crazy and she needed something to calm her ass down. I swear I thought about just slapping the shit out of her, but then I didn't want a fight to break out. There had to be some other way to get through to her. I just didn't know what it was.

"Why the fuck are you just standing there, Tyson?! Did you hear me?" Tray shouted walking over to the dresser to pick up a half smoked blunt. "I asked if you even care that your unborn child is dead?!"

"Yea, that shit fucked my head up and I'm hurt behind it, but this ain't the way to deal with it Tray!"

"Well, is this the way?" she snarled whipping out that 9mm she had purchased a couple of months ago. "Is this the way to end my pain? Is this what you want me to do?

Aiming the gun at me, Tray cried and cussed me out about any and everything. Honestly, I really wasn't paying attention to any of it. All I wanted was her to put that fucking gun down!

"Put it down Tray!"

"No! I'm not putting shit down! I can't have a baby by you, but Eraina can?! You can't be with me, but you're gonna be there for her and her baby! Is that what you think Tyson? You think I'm gonna stand around while you live happily ever after with that bitch? Or do you want this?"

Suddenly, Tray turned the gun on herself. My heart nearly beat out my chest thinking the worst. Now, I had no clue what was going through her head. Before I had a chance to do anything, she pointed the gun back at me. Only this time, her eyes were bugged out like a crazy person.

"YOU SON OF A BITCH!! YOU MADE ME LOSE MY BABY!!" she shouted angrily.

"Tray please put the gun down! I'm sorry!" Now, I realized the danger that I was in. When the hell did Tray become so unstable?

Sure, I knew she was upset about the baby, but I never thought she was this upset. She continued to point the gun at me as tears streamed down her face.

"Put the gun down bitch or I will blow this nigga's head clean the fuck off!" I heard someone say from behind me as I felt a cold piece of steel pressed against the back of my head.

"SHOOT HIM JOSE!! I DON'T GIVE A FUCK ABOUT HIM!!" Tray yelled. "THAT NIGGA DON'T WANT ME!!"

"Bitch you think I'm playing?" Jose asked as he cocked the hammer of his gun.

What did Tray do? She cocked the hammer of hers too. Oh my God! I just knew that I was about to die. I was standing in the middle of two fools with guns.

"I'm sorry Tyson," Tray apologized to me with tears streaming from her eyes. What the fuck was she apologizing to me for? Why did she say it like it was final or something?

I found that out soon enough. Next thing I knew...

POW!

I heard the loudest noise and felt the most awful pain before I hit the floor. I didn't know where I was hit, but I knew I had gotten struck by someone's bullet. The pain was intense. It felt like my whole body was on fire. All I could do was pray that I lived to see another day. While I was lying on the floor praying, I heard several more gunshots.

Before I closed my eyes, I saw Tray fall to the floor. I just hoped she was okay...

Chapter Twenty-Three

Trashelle

I had been going through the worst time of my life and I had no one to turn to. I had lost my precious little baby and hadn't heard from Tyson since we left the hospital. I knew that he blamed me for losing our baby and he was right... it was my fault. I didn't want to admit it at first, but over the past couple of weeks, all I could do was sit in this house and think. I came to the realization that if I hadn't gone to the club that night, my baby would still be safe inside my belly.

Tyson had every right to blame me because I blamed myself. I finally saw the truth and now I understood why he had stayed away from me. It still hurt like hell though. I guess if I didn't love him, it wouldn't have bothered me if he contacted me or not. But I loved that man. I loved him more than I loved myself.

When he called and said he was coming over, I rushed to the bathroom to try and make myself look decent. I hadn't bathed in at least a week. I hadn't been combing my hair or anything. The only thing I had been doing these past few weeks was existing.

Nonstop, I had been eating, drinking, and smoking. All I was trying to do was eliminate the pain that was etched in my heart from the loss of our baby. Why hadn't I stayed home that night?

Why did I have to put myself in danger when I knew that lunatic was still out there? I hated that I had put Tyson before my baby that night.

It was because of how Tyson had me feeling that made me leave the house that night. I should've just stayed my ass at home. I should've done that. Now I had nothing... no man, no baby, no one.

I stood in the bathroom looking at myself in the mirror unable to recognize who the fuck was staring back at me. Who was this chick with the matted hair, dirty face and sunken cheeks? I looked a hot mess and I had lost several pounds. Not to mention the fact that I had no color in my face at all. Maybe Tyson was right. Maybe I did need help.

While I stood there in the mirror lost in my thoughts, Tyson came busting through the bedroom screaming my name. That was when I produced the gun. I knew that my trusted friend Mag would take my pain away. I was going back and forth aiming the gun at Tyson, then myself until I saw Jose standing behind Tyson with a gun to his head.

All I saw in that moment was red. I didn't care if I lived or died anymore, but I loved Tyson. I wasn't about to let that fool kill the man that I loved. At first, I tried using reverse psychology on that fool by giving him permission to kill Tyson. But that fool didn't bite.

"SHOOT HIM JOSE!! I DON'T GIVE A FUCK ABOUT HIM!!" I hollered at the top of my lungs, hoping that my neighbor with the shotgun could hear me. "THAT NIGGA DON'T WANT ME!!"

"BITCH YOU THINK I'M PLAYING WITCHU?!!" Jose snarled as he cocked his hammer back. Shit, he wasn't the only one that knew how to cock a hammer, so I cocked mine while still pointing the gun at him.

"I'm so sorry Tyson," I said as I pulled the trigger.

I watched as Tyson fell to the floor, but that only held my attention for a minute as I fired the gun two more times before I felt an intense pain in my chest. I fell to the floor in a heap of funky mess. All I could think of was that I hoped I hadn't killed the man I loved. I was having trouble breathing, but it was okay. I was ready to go.

Life on this earth hadn't been good to me this past month, so I was ready to join my baby. I wasn't even fighting to breathe because if it was my time, it was just my time.

As a sudden calmness took over me, I looked at Tyson as he closed his eyes and mumbled the three words that I longed to hear him say... I love you.

Epilogue

Six months later...

Eraina

So much had happened over the past six months that sometimes I thought it was a dream. First off, I was still pregnant. I had less than two weeks left to go before I delivered my baby boy. I knew I was having a little boy, and I couldn't be happier. I knew he was going to look just like his daddy.

Tyson and I got married three months ago. I know, I was just as surprised when he asked me to be his wife. I guess getting shot and having his life flash before his eyes changed him. Hell, it changed me too!

When I heard that Tyson had been shot, I couldn't believe it. He had told me he was going to talk to Trashelle. How did talking end up in a shooting match inside her house?

So, apparently, the psycho dude who had been stalking her showed up and threatened to kill Tyson. In an effort to save Tyson, Trashelle shot him in the shoulder. His shoulder was messed up pretty badly, but he had been going to physical therapy and it was improving. At first, I was mad at her for shooting him, but once I heard the full story, I was grateful to her.

If she hadn't shot him first, that crazy nigga would've done it. Since Tyson had a gun to the back of his head, I doubted he would've survived that bullet. My baby would've had to grow up without a father.

Fortunately, that didn't happen and now I had the chance to step up. Since the shooting, I had been there for Tyson every step of the way. I really loved that man, and I proved it to him.

Now, I was living my dream with the man I loved and soon, we would be welcoming our son into the world. I had no one to thank for that but Trashelle.

Who would've ever thought?!

Nessa

So much shit had happened that I thought I'd never wake up from that nightmare. Finding out that Tyson had been shot six months ago was the worst thing my pregnant bestie could've ever gone through. I was there for her from the very beginning though. We weren't friends for nothing.

Proudly, I stood next to her when she and Tyson said their 'I do's' three months ago too. And I would be there for her when she gave birth to my godson. As for me, I had been going through crazy shit myself.

Sadly, I ended up having to testify against Byron for killing his wife and son. I couldn't believe he had actually gone through with it. It didn't even matter that I never wanted to see him again, even though he had told me in the beginning that was his reason for wanting to get rid of her.

Turned out, he wasn't even doing it for us to be together. He was doing it for the life insurance money. He had a policy on his wife worth $150,000 and the only way to cash it in was to kill her, so he did. I wished I had have done more to warn Regina that her life was in danger, but I didn't feel it was my place.

To be truthful, once several months went by and she was still alive, I thought Byron was just talking shit. But he actually went through with it. Now, his ass was sitting in state prison for the rest of his natural life, just rotting.

Well, when you did the crime, you had to do the time!

As I sat on the sofa, cuddled up next to the man my bestie recently hooked me up with, I thanked God that my life had changed for the better. From now on, I would no longer date married men.

If God says the same, I'm going to marry this one!

Tyson

Damn! That was all I could say about the past six months. When Tray shot me, I thought I was dead. All I knew was that she had pulled the trigger and shot me somewhere. The pain was so intense that I didn't realize where she shot me until after surgery when I opened my eyes and saw Eraina and my mom at my bedside.

What surprised me the most was that Trashelle had given up her life to save mine. She shot me then fired off two shots into Jose, but not before he was able to shoot one back at her. The bullet he fired, hit her dead in the chest. She died almost instantly. The two shots that she fired hit him in the head and neck. He died as soon as his body hit the floor.

Never in my life did I dream some shit like that would go down. I thought I was in the middle of a horribly scripted movie, but then I realized, it was actually my damn life that was playing out in front of me.

Woke my ass straight up! I mean, literally!

As soon as I opened my eyes and saw Eraina there, I knew what I had to do. Life was too short to be wasted. This woman was carrying my baby. She deserved to be my wife, so I asked her to marry me and she said yes. Three months later, we tied the knot with the justice of the peace in front of our family and closest friends.

Now, here we were, happier than I ever thought possible. I couldn't wait for our son to be born. I just wanted to hold him close, tell him that I loved him and teach him things. Especially what not to do when it came to women because my ex had certainly taught me a valuable lesson.

If it hadn't been for Trashelle, I'd most likely be pushing up daisies. I was definitely grateful to Tray for saving my life... even if it meant losing hers.

The end!!

CPSIA information can be obtained
at www.ICGtesting.com
Printed in the USA
LVHW041949061120
670968LV00003B/395